MW01594865

Surrendering to the Alpha

LIA DAVIS

Surrendering to the Alpha
An Ashwood Falls Novel
By: Lia Davis
Published by Fated Desires Publishing, LLC.
© 2013 Lia Davis

ISBN-13: 978-1-62322-057-0

Cover Art by Scott Carpenter

DEDICATION

To the love of my life.
Thanks for believing in me...

ACKNOWLEDGMENTS

I want to send a huge thank you to all my readers for making Ashwood Falls what it is today. Also thank you for all the kind words on Facebook and the emails. It is truly a pleasure to write this series.

Thank you, my always wonderful Street Team. You guys rock! Also sending a shout out to my assistant for all the hard work she does. I am enjoying working with her. And to my editors who are awesome.

A huge thanks to Carrie Ann for being my friend and business partner.

GLOSSARY

Alpha – Leader of the Pack

Marshal (First born no matter the sex) – Leader of the enforcers and sentries. The Marshal will also step in to aid the Alpha in his duties when needed. If there isn't an heir then a Marshal is appointed by the Alpha

Beta – Second born to the Alpha and/or second in command to the heir/Marshal. Generally takes care of Pack issues.

Enforcers – Enforces Pack laws and secures the safety of the Pack.

Sentries – Generally guards the outer boarders of the Pack property. They can be called in to aid an enforcer in fighting and enforcing the law.

Trackers – Skilled in tracking down rogues and eliminating them

Den mothers/maternal females – Strong and protective, yet not dominate by nature, they watch over the youth in the Pack. Generally works in the nursery and schools and other programs where the children and teens are concerned.

Justice – Pack lawyer with the special psychic ability to read memories through touch in order to place fair judgment on the accused and see the intent of outsiders that come to the den.

Empath – Can connect to the Pack though their emotions and offers comfort when needed and advices the Alphas and Marshals of potential issues between Pack members.

Scribe – Keeps the Pack history through the rare ability to pick up visions through touch. The ability works on objects and people. Many are loners and only like the company of other Scribes.

Rebels – There are two groups: shifters and humans. Shifter rebels had banned together to stop the Onyx and other rogues by force. Human rebels had banned together after discovering the shifter communities and seek to destroy all of them, good or bad.

Council of Elders – Past Alphas and Marshals that form a united ruling body over all Packs to ensure the laws of secrecy from humans are kept and enforced.

CHAPTER ONE

Thirty-seven years ago

Keegan opened the door to his home and was met with silence, although it wasn't unusual to come home from patrol to a quiet house or an empty one. Cate often visited with other Pack members and had her daily routines.

He stepped inside the foyer, taking in the scent of peaches and Cate. She hadn't been gone long, he guessed. Entering the kitchen, he felt his lips lift in a small smile as he saw the note on the counter.

Hello, Lover. I went for my walk early so we could have the evening to ourselves. Be back soon.

Love you always,
Cate

A wicked thought entered his mind involving Cate naked and panting beneath him.

He moved to the refrigerator, opened it, and assessed its contents with a frowned. There was an empty milk jug, jar of jelly, and several "mystery" items that he wouldn't open to save his mate's life. He closed the door and wondered why she hadn't gone shopping. It wasn't like her to forget things like that, or at least it wasn't until six months ago when they lost their third child.

Keegan shook his head, trying to ease the painful tightening in his chest and turned toward the living room.

A knock on the front door brought him up short. He wasn't expecting anyone. When he crossed the foyer and opened the door, he was surprised to see Brock, one of his sentries, on the other side.

"Brock." Keegan gave him a short nod and stepped aside so the male could enter.

The sentry came in and offered a wry smile. Keegan opened his telepathy to allow him to hear Brock's thoughts. All Keegan heard was Brock reciting Mary Had a Little Lamb over and over. Gritting his teeth, Keegan turned to the living room.

"What is bothering you, Brock?"

The male peered at him as if confused for a brief moment, then shrugged and looked away. Yeah, something was definitely up.

"How is Beth?"

Brock looked back at Keegan and smiled. "My mate is good. A little annoyed that Dani had put her on bed rest until after she delivers the cubs."

Keegan's heart warmed at the thought of new life. Beth and Brock were excepting their first...well, first set of cubs. Beth was due to deliver the twins in a few weeks and Danica, the Pack Healer, had put the female on light to no duty. Keegan could just imagine how stir crazy the dominant female was going.

"Brock?" Keegan asked when the male seemed to lose himself in thought, still reciting the damned nursery rhyme in his head.

"Huh? Oh. I was wondering if it would be okay if I take some time off rotation."

"Sure. Take as much time as you need. I have a few junior soldiers who need the experience."

Brock relaxed, but only a little. By the way the male rocked on his feet and peered around the room, Keegan knew something else was bothering the sentry.

"Speak your mind, Brock."

Brock swallowed, but met Keegan's gaze. "Is Cate home?"

Keegan didn't stop a low growl from escaping. "She is on her walk."

"I mean no disrespect. Beth and I love your mate and would never want to..."

"Speak," Keegan said through gritted teeth.

"Last week when Cate came to visit with Beth...well, my mate said Cate didn't smell right. Beth said she had a scent on her that was not Pack. I thought that my mate was just having one of those pregnancy side effects or something and paid it no mind." Brock fell silent.

Keegan counted slowly in his head before saying, "Continue."

Brock took a deep breath. "I saw Cate the other day, coming in from her walk and wanted to thank her for stopping by to visit with Beth. I smelt it, too."

Keegan was still counting, still trying to reign in his control and not hit the male standing in front of him for even suggesting what Keegan believed he was. Thoughts of that morning when he used his gift on Cate to ease a nightmare entered his mind. She was dreaming of the

Alpha of the rogue Pack Onyx. That couldn't be it. She was only having a dream, wasn't she?

Keegan studied Brock, who looked as pale as bleached sand. Keegan didn't blame the male for being nervous. After all, according to their laws, it was a crime to accuse the Alpha's mate of betrayal, or anything for that matter.

"What did you smell?"

Brock peered at his feet. "The scent of a rogue."

Keegan growled, making the male flinch slightly and reached out again to touch Brock's mind. This time the male let him in to search for the memory. Search for any hint of a lie. What he found made his heart ache and confused the hell out of him.

Brock believed what he said and was also confused by it.

Why would Cate have an encounter with the rogues and not mention it to him or the enforcers or sentries?

Keegan withdrew from the male's thoughts and turned toward the French doors that led to the backyard. "You are excused. Take all the time you need to be with your mate."

"Sir, I only told you because I was concerned. If she'd been fighting them on her own..."

Keegan peered at him from over his shoulder. "Thank you, Brock."

The male nodded and left Keegan alone with his thoughts. Over the past six months, and since they lost their third child after being attacked by a mutant—the half-human, half-animal pawns of the rogue Onyx Pack—Cate had fallen into a deep depression. She forgot things like buying food for the house, and her walks became a little longer each day. Most the time she'd return within an hour. Other times Keegan would have to go search for her only to find her swimming in the creek not far from the outer wards of Ashwood territory.

One thing he didn't consider until now was the possible reason why she trained with the soldiers. At first he thought it was to keep her mind busy. After all she had trained to be an enforcer as a teen and up until she became an adult and Keegan made his intensions of mating her clear.

Keegan hoped Cate had been using her walks and "alone time" to hunt down the rogues that took their child from them instead of betraying the Pack like her dream suggested. Both scenarios sent a jolt of panic though him that quickly turned to anger.

He'd told her of the dangers of fighting alone. Hell she knew the dangers from her own training and from being the Alpha's mate.

The front door opened making Keegan whirl around and cast a hard stare at his mate as she entered the living room. Her dark brown hair was pulled back into a ponytail and there was a hint of surprise in her grey eyes as she met his gaze.

"Oh, you're home." She smiled and moved to the hallway. "I'm going to shower and change then start dinner."

He was in front of her before she took her next step, drawing a gasp from her. He inhaled deeply, taking in her scent and the scent of a rogue. But not just any rogue, no it was Felix, the Onyx Alpha. The same man that order the attack on Ashwood and many other Packs in the southeast region of the United States.

The one male Keegan wanted to bring down and make suffer for destroying his Pack about two hundred years ago. The male that was responsible for the suffering of the members of Ashwood and the loss of his and Cate's little girl.

"What have you been up to, Cate?"

Fear entered her gaze and she swallowed, hard. Shaking her head, she backed away from him. "Nothing. I..."

Wrong answer.

He growled and stepped forward, his leopard rising to the surface. "Don't lie to me. I can smell Felix on you."

Tears sprang in her eyes and overflowed her lips to spill down her cheeks. "I'm so sorry," she said on a hiccup before she launched forward and grabbed his gun from his holster. Shock froze him in place for a brief moment, but it was all the lead she needed.

Cate flung the back doors open and ran toward the forest. Keegan gave chase. A blanket of fog drifted in heavy and thick in the darkening forest, making it hard to track by sight alone. He scented the air and picked up on her sweet, peachy scent.

His fear fueled the possessive rage building inside. She'd been with Felix.

Keegan couldn't shake the thought that she might have betrayed him. The thoughts he stole from her mind that morning fueled the panic that settled in his chest. His chest tightened and became hard to breathe through his own fear of what his mate might have planned to do with that gun. Shoving aside the sick feeling deep in his gut, he pushed his legs to run faster to catch her before she did something stupid.

"Cate!"

A twig snapped in the distance to his right, followed by a soft cry, and he turned toward it, desperate to reach her. When he broke through the thick brush, he saw her pushing herself up from the ground. Her watery gaze locked with his, and she raised her shaky hand with the gun in it and pointed it right at him.

He skidded to a stop and held his hands up, palms

facing her. "Cate, hon, we can talk about this. Whatever you've done, we'll work it out."

She shook her head, her long brown curls swaying around her shoulders. "I betrayed you and the Pack. I told Felix our secrets. I didn't mean to. I mean, I don't know why I did. I hate him. Oh, God, what have I done?" She broke out into sobs and looked away from him.

Keegan took a step forward. Cate snapped her gaze back to him and thrust the gun toward him in warning. "Stop. Don't, please. I must die. It's the law! I can't let you do it. I love you, and I'm so sorry for being a disappointment to you and the boys."

She moved the gun to her temple and Keegan screamed, "No," as she fired. He rushed over, catching her limp body, and fell to his knees with his dead mate pressed into his chest. Tears ran down his face and his chest felt like it was being pried open as he cried, hard. He let out a painful roar as he felt her soul rip from his own, severing their mating bond, leaving him empty and alone inside.

13

CHAPTER TWO

Present day

Keegan gasped as he sat straight up on the sofa he slept on. His body was covered in a sheen of sweat, and his heart pounded painfully behind his ribs. He scrubbed a hand over his face and peered around the room.

The safe house. He was in the safe house and not back in the woods the day Cate had died.

Fuck. It was just a dream.

No, a nightmare of a memory.

Pulling out his phone, he checked the time, and his eyes lingered on the date. No wonder he dreamed about that awful day. It was the thirty-seventh anniversary of her death.

What he still didn't understand was why. Why had she believed she had to die? There was always a loophole in the law. All she had to do is trust that they'd work it out.

She had believed death was the only punishment for her. He'd picked up on the thoughts that morning as he watched her sleep. It was the only time he was able to read her thoughts, although he never did it on purpose. He considered it too much of a violation of his mate's privacy. However, that morning, she'd muttered the word onyx. And after everything the rogue Pack had done to them, he couldn't stop himself from slipping into her thoughts. He opened his gift to ease the nightmare he believed she was having.

What he found tore his heart out. She talked with the Onyx Alpha as if they were friends, revealing that Keegan and Blaine would be away from the den that afternoon. It was never okay to reveal Pack secrets or any information to another Pack Alpha. To feed information to the one Alpha who wanted to destroy Ashwood and the other Packs in the southeast region of the United States, was an act of treason.

And punishable by death.

Fury mixed with hurt from her betrayal made him withdraw from her thoughts, and he'd pushed the emotions away and refused to believe that his mate would betray him. For all he knew, it could be her own mind creating the thoughts from a dream she had.

Regret washed over him. If only he'd woken her and asked her about it while he wasn't armed. Maybe he could have stopped her from ending her life...

The rustling of clothes and a soft shuffle of feet against the hardwood floors drew his attention to the opening of the hallway. Addyson Lewis, Pack Scribe, stood wringing her gloved hands in front of her. She'd changed her hair color again right before they'd come to cabin three days ago. The thick straight stands were now blond with purple streaks that made her violet eyes stand out more.

She was beautiful.

He peered into her worried gaze and offered a weak smile. The way she hung back, careful not to come too close to him, and the way she shifted nervously from foot to foot told him she'd sensed his dark mood. She smiled back in that timid way that said her snow leopard was a submissive, but she didn't move from the spot where she watched him.

Addyson fled to Ashwood just about twenty-five years ago when she'd escaped captivity from Onyx. Generally submissives weren't scared of others. Cautious, yes, but they didn't run unless the dominant pushed their cat into total submission. That was rare within a healthy pack because the submissive shifters were the ones to calm and bring peace to the dominants that protected them. They were the backbone of the Pack and a vital asset in keeping the balance within the den.

In Addyson's case, she'd had a hundred years of hell at the hands of Felix and his rogues. So, yeah, she had a right to be extra cautious.

With a sigh, he held out his hand. "Come here."

She stepped into the living room and sat in the chair across from him. He felt his lips twitch at her small defiance and dropped his hand. Leaning back on the sofa, he studied her closer. "Did I wake you?"

"No. I've been up for about an hour."

He frowned. It was still early morning, only 7:00. "Why didn't you wake me?"

She shrugged. "I read until I heard you stir." Her gaze drifted to his bare chest then back up to his face. A hint of pink colored her cheeks, and her strawberry scent intensified a little. She cleared her throat and asked, "Did you have a bad dream?"

He nodded, not wanting to lie to her. He never liked lies or sugarcoating shit. God knew there'd been enough of that shit while he'd been mated. With Addyson, Keegan knew that she preferred the ugliness along with the beauty that life offered. He was free to speak his mind without worrying about offending her or scaring the shit out her.

"Today is the anniversary of my mate's death."

Addyson didn't gasp like most submissive females would. Instead, her face softened in a caring way. Then again Addyson wasn't like any female he'd meet. "Thirty-seven years," she offered softly.

He nodded, not surprised she knew or remembered the date. She was a Scribe, and from what he understood about them, they never forgot anything. Besides the date of Cate's death was common knowledge within the den, and to most outsiders as well. Only everyone believed rogues had killer her. Shot in the head trying to save her mate.

Yeah, did he say he hated lies?

Well, some lies are meant to protect. This one held up the walls that blocked in the uncontrollable rage that lived inside him. The rage that had taken him three years to contain. The lie also honored her memory to the Pack that had loved her as much as he did, and still did.

"You care to talk about it?"

He snapped his gaze to Addyson's at the question. She was trying to help, and he so didn't need her kindness right now. "No."

Unfazed by the clipped word, she stood just as Will, the fifteen-year-old that had lead a group of rogue assassins into the den two months prior, walked in the living room. Will wasn't very tall, maybe five two at the most, and he was much too thin for a shifter his age. At first glance the teen looked to be around twelve. Although he had started to fill out in the months he'd been with Addyson.

The kid immediately went over to Addyson and hugged her. She froze for a moment then relaxed and wrapped her arms around him. Her expression softened almost as if relieved to have the touch of another shifter without pain. The two of them had explained that Scribes couldn't pick up on each other's psychic signatures.

It was one reason why Scribes didn't mate with other shifters and lived in pairs or groups within the den they were connected to.

Addyson and Will had both been ripped from their families and made to serve the rogues. They were forced to use their psychometric powers to pull secrets and histories from objects. Without the protection of another Scribe to buffer the ill effects caused by the emotional backlash from the visions they'd go insane. Keegan was amazed that Addyson hadn't lost her mind. Instead she lost the ability to shield the emotions and the pain that came with them.

Pulling back from the hug, Addyson ruffled the boy's blond hair and smiled. Will rolled his eyes playfully. Keegan felt his own lips lift at the exchange between the two. "What do you want for breakfast?"

Will stole a quick glance to Keegan before answering. "Can I have an omelet?"

Addyson smiled and nodded. "Sure, hun."

Keegan watched her and Will walk toward the kitchen, which was a few feet away. When they were out of eyesight, he dropped his head into his hands. What the fuck was he doing?

He was hiding out in a two-bedroom cabin in the mountains.

This was crazy. He was the Alpha, damn it. Well at least until he transferred the power to his eldest son in a few hours.

He'd brought Addyson and Will to the safe house to protect them. He was sure Onyx would look for Will or at least discovered that Addyson was alive.

He stood and made his way to the kitchen, leaned on the doorframe, and watched Addyson carefully flip the omelet. Her blond and purple hair was now tied back with a black ribbon. She was smiling, making her look angelic and otherworldly, almost elfin. As if sensing him, she lifted her gaze and met his stare. Her smile faded, and disappointment washed over him.

He stepped closer and studied her as she turned back to the omelet. Keegan ground his molars, took a deep breath, and calmly asked, "Do you like it here?"

She peered back at him, her eyebrows bunched together before she smoothed out her features in that practiced control she used around others. "It's not home, but it's nice. I don't need much, Keegan."

He took another step toward her. She turned the stove off and handed Will his plate. The boy stood, watching Keegan as if he would harm Addyson. It made Keegan proud of the kid that he'd want to protect her.

Without looking at the teen, Keegan said, "Will, take your breakfast in the living room and eat before it gets cold."

From the corner of his eye, Keegan saw Will peer at Addyson. When she gave him a nod, he left them alone. Keegan took another step forward, stopping inches from her. He heard her heart beat speed up and smelled her strawberry scent intensify, but not in fear. She was turned on by his presence.

He inhaled deeply, taking in her scent. His leopard rubbed up against his chest, trying to feel Addyson. He'd never imagine in the past thirty-seven years that he'd find another mate. Then Addyson stumbled into his life about twelve years after losing Cate. He wasn't ready then, the pain still too raw to acknowledge what the leopard tried to make him see.

He'd finally started to accept it, accept the fact that Addyson had a place in his heart and in his bed.

That was exactly where he wanted her every night.

"I have to leave," he said in a low whisper.

Her shoulders dropped, and she let out a sigh. "I know."

"There will be two sentries, Tanner and Kirk, coming to watch over the cabin. I have to go to the den and transfer the Alpha power to Blaine." He watched her eyes shift from deep purple to almost a lavender as she studied him for several moments. God, he wished he could read her thoughts, but her mind was one of the few he couldn't enter. Not even in sleep. He'd tried once, about a year after she'd arrived at Ashwood, but it wasn't for selfish reasons. He'd wanted to help her mind heal from the trauma she endured at the hands of Felix and his rogue den.

She didn't have any mental shields, yet she was unreadable to him. In fact his whole telepathic ability seemed to dull around her.

She narrowed her eyes and said, "You're not coming back."

He sighed. "Not here. Tanner and Kirk will move you and Will to a new location. Can you make sure you're ready at a moment's notice?"

"Of course. Do you expect an attack?"

He gave a nod, and she removed the glove from her right hand and cupped his cheek. They'd discovered a couple of months ago when he visited with her to see if she could pick up something from a journal that belonged to Graham's ex-lover, that his touch didn't hurt her. Addyson had a way to read an objects energy without touching it. That way she'd know if the object held dark emotions and could gage how much it would hurt to read the object. When she went to stand to get him a drink, he grabbed her arm to stop her. She'd said she hadn't had a vision when he touched her. Even though he was still careful with her, he could sense that his gentleness annoyed her at times. Yet he still didn't understand why his touch didn't affect her. Why she couldn't read his psychic energy like she did others.

Looking into her violet eyes, he asked, "Is this causing you pain?"

"No. It's like when I touch Will. There's no transfer of energy at all." She averted her gaze shyly and he had the urge to kiss her.

"Are you sure?"

"Yes."

Closing his eyes, he covered her hand with his and pressed his forehead to hers. Complete silence and calm. He didn't understand how her touch could shut off the low hum inside his head due to his telepathic abilities, but he was selfish enough to enjoy it.

"Be safe, my Alpha," she whispered then pulled away and lowered her eyes so he couldn't see her face.

He didn't have to see the emotions she tried to hide behind that wall of control she clung to. He could smell them. Fear and sadness were a mixture of sour and sweet that came together like spoiled fruit. His leopard growled and clawed beneath his skin, wanting out so he could comfort the broken female in front of him.

No, Addyson wasn't broken. She was scarred on the inside so deeply that she hid from the world around her.

Why? Keegan didn't know for sure. He might be the only one, besides Rhea, the head den mother that ran the nursery, and Shayna, Keegan's daughter, that were close enough to Addyson to be considered her friends, but that didn't mean he knew anything about her. Sure he knew she'd spent most of her life held captive by Onyx, and they'd forced her to use her psychic gifts to feed them information—like which Packs were the weakest and any Pack secrets she could glean from stolen items.

When her mind finally broke, tearing down all her natural shields that protected her from the painful emotions she received from her visions, and she was of no use to Onyx anymore, they set her free, only to hunt her down like an animal.

Keegan ground his molars together at the memory of the day he'd found her, beaten, bloodied, and crazed out of her mind. She'd crossed over Ashwoods' wards as she ran from the mutants hunting her. Keegan's sentries and enforcers destroyed the half-animal assassins while he wrapped Addyson in a blanket and brought her to his home, where he discovered that he couldn't read her thoughts, nor could he help repair her mind.

She had to do that on her own.

Coming out of the past, he studied her for a moment, then asked, "Will you be okay while I'm gone?"

She cut her gaze to him. "I'm not a child. I'll be fine." She lifted her chin and left the kitchen.

He couldn't stop the smile from forming on his lips as she walked away from him. She had a hidden fire inside her, and he was going to enjoy bringing it out.

****

Addyson sagged in relief as a knock sounded on the door and drew Keegan's attention away from her before he could chase her down. He was too close in the kitchen. His heat caressed over her body in sensual waves, calling to her. She had the overwhelming need to rub up against him like a needy house cat just to see if a full body skin-on-skin shorted out her senses. It'd been way too long since she'd let another touch her or even be as close as Keegan had been the last few weeks.

God, his wild, earthy scent drove her mad.

She peered at the door as Keegan opened it to the two young sentries. Each nodded to Keegan in greeting then flicked their gazes to her. Tanner Raines, Luna's youngest son, offered her a gentle smile. She relaxed a little more.

Tanner was a strong, yet quiet, wolf. He was also very handsome like his brothers, Dane and Hayden. Tanner's dark auburn hair fell over his ears and reached his jaw line, framing his young face. His boyish good looks and his quiet nature told nothing of the power inside him.

He was telekinetic—able to move and control objects with his mind—and from what Addyson heard, his ability was very powerful. Shay, Keegan's daughter, had told her once that Tanner's gift went beyond just moving objects. He could bend them, break them, and even shatter glass with his mind.

She smiled back at Tanner then at Kirk, who was always a little too serious. "Hello, boys."

Kirk grunted, but she swore she caught a slight twitch at the corner of his mouth. The sentry was a leopard shifter. Underneath that hard exterior, he had a gentle soul. His family had survived the first wave of attacks on Ashwood over two hundred years ago. He'd been there when Keegan found her outside the den. God, how long ago had it been? Twenty-five years, give or take.

"I'm hardly a boy, ma'am." Kirk took a step toward her with his hand raised as if he was going to touch her. It was an automatic response for shifters. In fact touch was as important to them as breathing. When they greeted a fellow Pack member it was customary to touch a hand or shoulder.

It was something Addyson couldn't allow no matter how much she craved it.

She took a step back and Keegan moved to stand in Kirk's path, halting him and drawing his gaze from her to his Alpha. A moment later Kirk lowered his head in a submissive way.

Addyson's heartbeat kicked up for several beats. None of the sentries or the enforcers was submissive by any means. Each one held a dominant power that was unique.

She wanted to tell Keegan it was okay, but she remained motionless. Mistakes like the one Kirk was about to make could get him killed. And not from the Alpha who protected her in a way she didn't quite understand.

No, in the field, if Kirk forgot the dangers for even a split second, he'd lose his life.

With his head still lowered, he lifted his gaze to hers as if waiting for her reaction and spoke to the Alpha. "I will go back to the den and have Blaine send a replacement."

Silence filled in the space around them for far too long. Addyson wasn't sure how much longer she could stand it. The childish urge to knock over furniture or a lamp or something to break the silence made her palms itch. She'd had enough of the cold quiet during her hundred years as the Onyx's pet.

Finally Keegan spoke, easing her tension a little. "Be

at ease. Your comfort with Addyson is the reason you're here. However, be warned that if you forget about what touch can do to her again, you will know exactly what she feels."

Kirk lifted his gaze to meet Keegan's and nodded. "Understood."

The sentry didn't even flinch at the warning. However, she did, even though she knew that the Alpha was law and if he didn't have a handle over his soldiers, then he'd be seen as weak.

She stepped forward until she was a foot from Keegan and offered her gloved hand, first to Tanner then to Kirk. Each gently squeezed her hand before releasing it. She dropped her hand. "Thanks for babysitting me."

She didn't bother keeping the annoyance out of her tone. She was still mad at Keegan's too-careful, too-fathering tone in the kitchen. She wasn't a child, damn it. She sure wasn't some helpless submissive that needed coddling.

When she was around Keegan, she had an uncontrollable urge to spar with him, in more ways than one. The male just brought out a side of her she didn't recognize. A side that was a little naughty. She wanted to misbehave so he'd stalk her and make her be good.

Keegan turned to face her, and she knew her skin was flashed from the thoughts running in her mind. His brown eyes narrowed as if he was trying to read her, but she didn't feel the dull pressure that usually came with a telepath shifting through her thoughts. After a few moments he lifted his hand, knuckles facing her as though he was going to caress her cheek, but he dropped his hand and stepped away from her.

She frowned. She'd thought Keegan had shared the information that he could touch her. Pushing away the tinge of hurt she had no right to feel, she turned her attention to Will, who came up beside her and wrapped an arm around her waist. She smiled at him and ran a hand over his hair.

Keegan touched her gloved hand tentatively, and she lifted her gaze to meet his. "Be ready in an hour."

At first, his statement confused her, and then she remembered what he'd said in the kitchen. Tanner and Kirk were moving her and Will to a new location.

"I will. Thanks."

Keegan stared into her eyes for several moments before he turned, walked out the door, and disappeared into the forest surrounding the cabin.

Her heart ached as she suddenly felt alone. She pushed the feeling away, straightened her shoulders, and studied the sentries still standing on the front porch. "What now?"

Tanner cleared his throat. "Umm, we'll just search the perimeter until it's time to go." He spoke low enough that only the four of them could hear, most likely in the event spies were lurking about.

She nodded, and Kirk held out a small walkie-talkie. She motioned to Will next to her. "Give it to Will." Even though she could take the device with her gloves on, she just didn't fell like dealing with it. No, she had to think of a way to break down the walls around Keegan's heart.

Kirk handed the walkie-talkie to Will without question, and the two sentries took off in separate directions.

Addyson slid the door back into place and dropped her shoulders. There was something Keegan wasn't telling her. She could feel it in the air, a muted electric current that had nothing to do with the desires Keegan rose in her. No, this energy was dark and evil.

There was something out there. Something waiting

for them to make their move.

"I'm picking up on something dark," Will said.

Addyson ran a hand through his blond hair and rested it on his shoulders. "So am I, hon. I feel it, too."

CHAPTER THREE

Keegan turned the Jeep onto the narrow dirt road that appeared to humans like a walking trail. Once he drove through the wards surrounding Ashwood Falls, the path opened up to a road that was big enough for one vehicle at a time. He didn't have to worry about humans too much. The wards gave them a false sense of unease, making them turn away from the property. In many places, like entry points, the wards also held an illusion spell that changed roads to foot trails and buildings appeared to be run-down.

The wards also served as an alarm system of sorts. Keegan and his enforcers and sentries would instantly know if anyone crossed through them with the intent to harm.

It didn't, however, stop Onyx from sending their soldiers to test out the added security.

No, the rogue bastards didn't care. They'd come through them anyway and meet with the force of Ashwood's sentries, who wouldn't hesitate in the slightest to bring down any threat to the Pack.

Over the last few months, Keegan and Blaine along with Luna—the wolf Alpha—and her son, Hayden had worked to increase the security around the perimeter of Ashwood Falls' territory. They'd doubled the amount of sentries on patrol by putting their strongest soldiers on rotation.

He rolled to a stop at the security gate, and Alec, his youngest son, stepped out of the small building, gave him a nod, and then opened the gate. Keegan waited for his son to come around to the passenger side and climb into the Jeep before stepping on the gas.

Alec punched him on the shoulder. "'Sup, Pops."

Keegan laughed and grabbed Alec's forearm, relishing the instant connection to his son. God, he'd missed his sons and Shay. A weaker shifter would have gone crazy without his Pack for two weeks.

This whole thing sucked sewer water, but his plan had to work. He gave Alec's arm a little squeeze, then drove through the gate, taking the left toward his home. "It feels good to be here."

Alec growled and turned to peer out the window. "I don't like this plan of yours. We should stand together, whole like the powerful Pack we are."

Keegan ignored Alec's growl of disapproval as he pulled into the driveway of his house. Blaine's truck, along with Cameron's and Graham's cars, was parked under the carport. He lifted a brow at Alec. "I take it I no longer have a home."

Alec grinned. "The trio and I swapped. I'm staying

at Cam's old apartment. The house has more room for the kids."

Besides the house isn't the same without you here.

Keegan caught Alec's thought, knowing his son had deliberately left his mental shields down, the shields that blocked Keegan from "picking his brain," as Alec usually called it.

His chest tightened.

Yeah, this sucked.

The front door opened, and Blaine stepped out with Max, his three-year-old stepson, on his hip. Keegan smiled at the sight. He knew one day Cam and Blaine would bless him with grandchildren, but the sight of Blaine holding the small boy still amused Keegan. His eldest son was such a hardass that he forgot the softer side that Blaine showed only to his family.

Shutting off the engine, Keegan opened the car door and stepped out, and a smile spread wide on his face. He couldn't stop the smile if he'd wanted. It felt too damn good to be home, even if it seemed his house had been taken over.

Blaine pulled him into a one-arm hug. Keegan hugged him back, tight. He inhaled, taking in the scents of home and family. He was doing the right thing. The transfer of power was for the better of the Pack. They'd all be stronger for it. All he could do was pray that he wasn't setting himself up and walking into a trap.

Tiny tugs at his long black hair drew his attention to Max. The toddler grinned at him, his blue eyes bright. Keegan touched a finger to Max's cheek. "Hi, little man."

"Hi, Grandpa."

Surprise hit him and quickly turned to a mushy lump in his chest.

Fuck.

Blaine clasped him on the shoulder. "We're at war.

It's time to shift power and tactics."

Keegan peered into his son's eyes and held his gaze for a long moment. He was right. Blaine was one in a triad, a very powerful triad that would provide the Pack with the will and strength they needed to win this war.

With a nod, Keegan agreed. "You're right. Seven hundred years is a long time to be Alpha." He offered a lazy grin that made Blaine roll his eyes as he lowered Max to the ground.

Blaine popped Max on the butt gently and said, "Go find your sister and get ready for the party."

Max let out a squeak then laughed while babbling "party" over and over as he toddled off into the house. Keegan's smile widened, and he shook his head. "Fatherhood fits you."

Blaine turned to peer into the house, which was possible because Max had left the front door wide open. "Yeah. Those kids are great. Max is hell on wheels, and Sammie is so smart." Blaine narrowed his eyes and crossed his arms over his chest. "Have you heard from K?"

Keegan shrugged and held Blaine's stare. "About three weeks ago." Blaine set his jaw, making a tic form in his temples, and raised a brow in an 'I'm listening' kind of way. Keegan let out a sigh. "It wasn't face-to-face. He left me a message at the usual place that said there was something worth my attention."

Blaine growled low and spoke through clenched teeth. "You're doing this just to go into Onyx on a wild goose chase?"

Keegan growled back and inched closer to his son. "I'm doing this to protect the Pack, Addyson, and Will. I'll find out what the source has to report and decide then."

Blaine inhaled deeply and blew out the breath. "He

didn't tell you what it was?"

Of course Keegan's spy had told him, but he wasn't about to share the information with Blaine, at least not yet. "Nope, but I'll find out and then decide if it's worth pursuing."

Keegan turned to go inside the house, stopping any other questions Blaine might have about the spy Keegan had placed inside the Onyx Pack almost ten years ago. It was risky, but worth it. In the beginning, they'd received good intel on the Pack structure and valuable information on the mutants, the creatures that were forever frozen in mid-shift.

However, in recent years, the lines of communication were becoming further and further apart. In fact, three weeks ago was the first time Keegan had heard from the spy since nine months before.

Stepping into the living room, Keegan smiled at Cam lying against Graham's chest and Max curled up in her lap. They were watching some cartoon show. Keegan's chest tightened again.

He missed the days when the kids were small and he and Cate had cuddled on the sofa while the boys played on the floor or sat with them to watch a movie.

The memory of him holding Cate against his chest while he rubbed her pregnant belly flashed in his mind. She'd been six and a half months along with their third child. A girl, according to Dani. They'd given up hope in having another child. Their sons were grown and had been in their Pack roles for well over a decade before Cate got pregnant. They were excited beyond belief when they found out. He and Cate had sat on the sofa and watched Blaine and Alec discussing enforcer training exercises. They were arguing over how to make them more challenging.

Cate loved throwing in completely off-the-wall

suggestions, making them all laugh.

He broke off the memories and walked to the kitchen to grab a beer out of the fridge. He couldn't let himself to go there. It was too painful because that night had been the start of the end.

After dinner, Cate had gone on her walk like she had every night since he'd known her. She was very independent, and Keegan respected that half of her. Besides it gave her the much-needed time to be without the pressures of the Pack and being the Alpha's mate.

When she didn't return in her normal thirty-minute timeframe, he got worried and set out to search for her. It had taken him only a few seconds to reach her. She lay on the ground in a ball, covered in blood, and sobs shook her body.

Dread and fear like nothing he'd ever felt before cut through him as he lifted her in his arms and rushed her to the medical center. Her pain was almost too much for him to take.

It was an agonizing hour later that Cate's nurse came out to tell him the baby had died.

Damn it.

He shook his head to clear his thoughts. He clenched the bottle so hard he swore he heard it crack. Damn K for bringing back one of the memories Keegan had buried a long-ass time ago.

The spy had said that Keegan's daughter hadn't died, and K had proof she was still alive and living inside the Onyx den.

His curiosity had gotten the better of him. It was most likely going to hurt like hell, but he couldn't walk away if he wanted to. He had to know if his daughter was still alive and bring her home. Where she belonged.

Thirty minutes later, Keegan stood inside the Pack circle with Blaine and Luna, the wolf Alpha and co-

Alpha to Ashwood Falls. Her long red hair was braided down her back, and her green eyes held wariness in them. She didn't like Keegan's plan. She'd told him as much several times, but she also said she'd stand by his decision.

Luna stepped forward and spoke low enough that only the three of them could hear. "Are you sure you know what you're doing?"

He held his hand out, palm up. She hesitated, but placed hers over his. He circled his fingers around her hand. "I'm certain. I'm tired, and Blaine, with his mates, are much stronger than I am."

She tugged her hand from his and stepped back. "I don't believe you, but I trust you."

He smiled at the thought she sent him. "Thank you, Lu."

She snorted at the nickname he always used when she tried to be stern with him. He studied her as she moved to stand beside him and faced the crowd. Luna had fast become a great friend. He was glad she'd had his back over the past thirty years as they'd built a solid Pack out of two broken ones. A Pack that no one thought would work because wolves and leopards were generally rivals and not allies.

"Hello, all my beautiful people, felines, and wolves." Luna's voice rang into the sunny afternoon, quieting the conversations around them. "Today marks a new beginning. Keegan Andrews, leopard Alpha for a little more than seven hundred years, is passing his legacy down to his eldest son, his Heir, Blaine. Keegan will take his place as an elder and adviser for the Pack."

Keegan felt his lips twitch. Leave it up to Luna to keep him at the top of the Pack's hierarchy. Elders were past Alphas, Marshals, and other titled Pack members who'd passed their positions and powers to their successors. In the old days, before the war with Onyx, the elders had sat on a council that kept the histories of all Packs and enforced the few, but important, rules they must follow.

The number one rule was secrecy from humans.

Luna turned to face him and took both his hands in hers. "It's been a pleasure ruling beside you over the years. Thank you for everything you've done for my wolves and opening your doors to merge the two Packs."

Keegan squeezed her hands gently and spoke to the Pack. "I know this may come at what seems the worst possible time. However, I believe that it is a positive step into the future. I may be stepping down from Alpha of Ashwood, but I will be taking the first seat of the Council of Elders in over two hundred years. We will rebuild what was lost and gain the advantage in this war. It's not going to be easy, and it won't happen overnight, but I'm not going to lie down and allow Onyx and their supporters win."

A rain of whoops and cheers poured from the Pack members standing around the circle. Power rose up all around him, warm and electrifying. With it came the unconditional love and respect each one had for their Alphas. His chest tightened, and a lump formed in his throat. They might still have issues between the younger wolves and leopards, but it was times like this that reminded him those differences were a part of growing and learning to trust one another.

Keegan stepped back so he could move to stand behind Blaine. Gripping his son's biceps, Keegan leaned in and whispered, "Whatever you do, don't fight it." Blaine's muscles tensed under Keegan's hold, and he smirked.

The warning he gave Blaine was more than his own father had given him. Keegan wasn't always an ass.

Keegan shifted his legs so they were spread apart to balance his weight evenly. Blaine was about three inches shorter than him, which would make this transfer a lot easier for both of them. Taking a deep breath and exhaling, Keegan spoke so the Pack could hear. "Blaine Andrews, Heir of the Ashwood Leopard Pack, do you accept the burdens, challenges, and full responsibility of being our Alpha?"

Blaine stood a little taller and lifted his chin. "I accept."

"Will you be their judge, executioner, friend, and father?"

Without hesitation, Blaine answered loud and proud as the born alpha male he was. "I will be all those things and more."

Keegan struck hard and fast, sinking his elongated fangs into Blaine's shoulder while wrapping an arm around Blaine's chest to keep the male from jerking away. Blaine hissed out a curse, and Keegan tightened his grip in warning.

The hairs on his arms stood on end as power washed over both of them. The air around them was alive with magick and coiled around them, nipping at their skin and putting their cats on edge. Keegan could sense both their leopards now. They growled and fought for dominance, raising even more power in thick warm waves. The struggle for power lasted several long moments. Keegan thought it'd never end. Finally Keegan's cat backed off to allow the magick that had passed down from his father, the power that made him Alpha, flow into Blaine. His son's breathing came in shallow pants as his body shook at the rush of new power.

It might have been over seven hundred years, but Keegan hadn't forgotten how it felt— first the pain of the bite then the burn of Alpha magick as it raced through him, seeping into every fiber of his and his leopard's soul.

Keegan on the other hand felt drained, almost empty inside. He still had his strength and natural abilities, but the Alpha power, the magick of the Pack was dulled. The heavy weight of sadness settled upon him. He could no longer feel the souls within the Pack.

After what seemed like an hour, Blaine stilled and sagged against him. Keegan took his son's weight and staggered back a step. He lifted his eyes to Cam and Graham and gave a short nod.

They rushed forward and helped Blaine balance on his feet. Blaine instantly drew his mates to him, and Keegan knew he was using the mating bond to center the new power flowing through his veins.

Blaine met his stare and grinned. "You okay?"

Keegan steadied himself. "Never better. A little lightheaded, but just fucking peachy." He turned to the Pack and held a hand out to Blaine, who was wrapped up in both his mates' arms. "Your new Alpha."

Wolves howled and cats roared their approvals, and that was Keegan's cue to start heading to the new safe house. He clasped Blaine on the shoulder and gave a nod to Alec, who stood at the circle's edge, scanning the forest for threats.

Alec would become Marshal, but the announcement would come as soon as Blaine chose a new Beta to replace him. Since Keegan didn't have any other children or blooded relatives inside the Pack, it was up to Blaine to appoint one. Usually it'd be someone already connected to him through the Alpha bond, such as an enforcer.

As he stepped outside the circle, Luna fell into step with him. "How long will you be gone?"

He shrugged. "Not sure. Kieran found something

that I need to look into." He held up a hand. "Don't ask. I can't share any more info right now. If it turns out to be a threat to the Pack, I'll let you know."

She made a low growl but didn't press for any more information. "Be safe."

He stopped and turned to her. "All I need is to make sure Addyson and Will are off Felix's radar, and then we'll return."

She averted her gaze to peer at the Pack circle. Worry creased her forehead as she scanned the area like the mama wolf she was. He frowned. Luna had the gift of visions, although she called it more of a curse. She didn't have control over what she saw, and no one outside of her family or his knew about her powers.

"You had a vision?" he asked.

She met his gaze and nodded. "It's the worst one I've ever had. Worst than the attacks on my den."

"Fuck."

"Yep. Felix is plotting something big. Maybe not now, but something is coming." To others, the fear in her tone would have been seen as a weakness. Keegan saw it as an emotion from an Alpha who would do anything for her Pack.

"Tell Blaine about the vision and start preparing and keep me posted."

She gave a nod and turned to walk back to the circle.

Keegan fisted his hands. Shit just kept getting deeper, and Keegan was going to get to the bottom of it in the next meeting with his spy.

CHAPTER FOUR

Addyson stood in the living room of the new safe house peering around in awe. They were inside a cave. It was unbelievable. It even had lighting, furniture, and a small kitchen to the right. There were three openings in the wall in front of her like separate passageways, or were they other rooms?

The trickling of water from somewhere deeper in the cave echoed off the walls. It wasn't loud. In fact it was barely audible, just enough to be soothing.

She took a deep breath, drawing in the cool, damp scents of sand, rock, and earth. This was heaven. The best part was she could touch the walls and walk around barefooted. The rock couldn't absorb emotions or psychic impressions.

Addyson walked over to the sofa and held her hand

over the cream-colored fabric and hesitated. Footsteps behind her made her turn to see Tanner standing at the opening of the cave. He smiled at her. "Only Keegan has been in here."

She stilled and looked around. There were no personal effects. "Why would he have this and not enjoy it?" she wondered aloud.

"He built it for Cate."

Addyson whirled around and frowned. "What?"

Tanner paled. "I shouldn't have said anything. I'm just going to go jump off the mountain now."

"Oh, no, you don't. Tell me." It came out as a demand, and it was a shame Keegan wasn't here to witness the backbone she suddenly had.

Tanner peered down at his boots. "I don't know for sure. It's all hearsay. Some rumors say he made a cavern getaway for the two of them right after they lost the baby..."

She held up a hand, stopping him. "Wait. What baby?"

He peered behind him at Kirk, as if asking for help. When Kirk shook his head and propped up against the stone doorway, Tanner muttered a curse and continued. "Cate had some kind of accident or something and lost the baby about six months before she died. No one speaks of it. Not even Blaine and Alec."

Addyson's vision blurred, and a lump lodged in her throat. She sat down on the sofa and studied her hands in her lap. She knew from personal experience that losing a mate was beyond devastating, but to also lose a child? She couldn't even imagine.

Will came over and sat next to her. "Addy?"

She reached over and covered his hand with hers. "Yes?"

"Do you want to practice shielding?"

She looked at him then smiled. He knew she needed a distraction from her thoughts. Learning how to shield herself from the emotions of others and their history would be wonderful, and it was a great way to pass the time until Keegan got back.

"Sure. What do I need to do?"

Will scanned the room before he stood and asked Tanner, "Can you move the couch so we all can sit on the floor?"

Tanner frowned. "We?"

The teen nodded. "Yes. She can't learn how to build shields if she doesn't have anyone to practice on."

Kirk snorted. "Yeah, right. And when Keegan gets back, he'll kick our asses."

Addyson glared at them. Okay, so maybe Keegan would be a little angry to find the sentries inside the cave with her. She stood and propped her fist on her hips, trying her best to look intimidating. Well as intimidating as a submissive snow leopard could. "Wouldn't he want me to find a way to protect myself?"

Tanner frowned, making his forehead wrinkle. "Yes, but—"

"And he would want me to do this with people I trust."

Kirk cleared his throat. "Addyson, my past...well, it's a little dark."

She paused, searching Kirk's face for a hint of teasing, but it wasn't there. Instead, a shadow moved in, and then fear crossed his face. He was afraid of hurting her and afraid of what Keegan would do if he did. She dropped her gaze and whispered, "Darker than the things I'd seen in my hundred years of captivity with the Onyx Pack?"

Tanner growled. The low rumble echoed off the cave walls. "A hundred years?"

41

She nodded. "It's why my mind is so broken." She gestured to Will standing next to her. "He's also a Scribe. He's not at full power yet, but he can shield against unwanted emotions that come with the visions."

Will grabbed her hand. "I can control when I want the visions, too."

Kirk shifted uneasily from leg to leg. "I'm guessing Will can help you shield."

Addyson nodded. "Yes." She hoped so anyway. If this worked, then she wouldn't have to hide in her house or wear the cloak and gloves when she went out. "Will you do it?"

Tanner blow out a breath and nodded. "Kirk and I need to do a perimeter check." He peered over her shoulder, and she heard the couch slide across the floor. He grinned, stepped outside with Kirk, and slid the large stone slab of a door into place.

She smiled and almost felt giddy. She was also scared shitless. Pivoting, she met Will's raised eyebrows. Oh, great, even at fifteen, he was trying to intimidate her. She let out a soft laugh. "You may be more dominant than me, but I'm older."

Will pressed his lips together as if hiding a smile from her. Addyson laughed. Man, it felt good to be around someone she couldn't pull psychic energy, which always left her a trembling mess on the floor.

She shivered at the thought and looked around the room again.

He tapped her on the arm, drawing her attention back to him. "The natural floors of the cave will help ground you."

She nodded. "Yeah, I know." She was still nervous. What if she found out her mind was too broken to create shields?

Will rolled up the area rug and sat down, folding his

legs like a pretzel. She sat next to him just as the sentries walked through the door. Kirk walked right over and dropped to the floor in front of her. Tanner was a little more hesitant and opted for the space between Kirk and Will.

Addyson took a deep breath and exhaled slowly. "How do we do this?"

Will shifted beside her so his body was turned to hers. "Close your eyes, clear your mind, and then ground yourself."

Okay, that was easy. She had to meditate on a regular basis in order to keep the monsters in her head at bay. She closed her eyes and imagined she sat by a small stream. Water trickled by her, soothing her. The air was clean, crisp, and held a hint of roses that reached her senses with each gentle breeze.

Most people visualized made up places, unique to only them in order to fully relax enough to ground themselves. Not Addyson. Her mind was filled with so much evil and ugliness that no one should ever have to witness. She visualized a real place. Somewhere she visited often and loved.

The stream, in reality, was located about one hundred yards from her backyard in Ashwood. It was her favorite place, so whenever she needed to relax, or calm her inner demons, she'd go to the stream and take in the beauty.

Now she went there in her mind because it was the only pure thing she knew.

Her muscles relaxed as a calm she hadn't felt since leaving her home in Ashwood a few weeks ago washed over her. She gathered all the negative, dark energy into a ball in the middle of her chest and slowly pushed it out. When the dark energy reached her hands and feet, she placed her palms on the cool stone floor and pushed it into the rock, imagining it being absorbed into the earth beyond.

She opened her eyes to see Tanner and Kirk staring at her. Self-conscious, she averted her gaze to Will. The teen quickly motioned to Tanner. "Give me your hand."

Tanner drew his brows together but placed his hand over Will's. The younger male smirked. "Were you ever a serial killer?"

Addyson held back a grin at Will's teasing tone. Tanner's lips twitched, but he kept all other emotions from his features. "I'm a sentry. I kill for a living."

Will laughed and lifted his hand so his palm touched Tanner's.

The muscles in Will's arm gave a little jerk at first, and Addyson wondered how bad it would be for her. After a few moments, Will withdrew his hand from Tanner's and turned to her.

"Since you told me your shields are completely gone, I want you to try to see if you can build them using his aura," Will said like it was no big deal.

Well, it might not be for him, but Addyson was trembling inside.

"Wait? Use his aura? How?"

Will bunched his eyebrows together. "It's one of the first techniques I learned when I came into my power."

"Okay," she said. She wasn't sure she ever learned that style of building or rebuilding shields. She tried to think back to her training as a child. She came up against a dark wall. No, it was more like a black void. Her memories of her childhood were gone.

Sadness filled her heart, but she knew she'd lost the ability to hold on to her past before her captivity. A warm tear rolled down her cheek.

Will took her hand in his. "Addyson?"

She lowered her gaze and focused on the stone floor

beneath her bare feet. "I don't remember how," she whispered.

Will squeezed her hand gently and said, "Use your second sight to see your aura, then expand yours out to his, but don't let your energies touch. Change your aura color to match his then bring it back to you. Your instincts should take over from there."

Addyson wasn't so sure about that, but she trusted Will. After all, he'd escaped Onyx with his mind intact. Taking a deep breath, she focused on Tanner and held her hand up between them. "Hold your hand up like mine, but don't touch mine."

He did as she asked. She closed her eyes and pushed her aura into his.

She opened her second sight, or mind's eye, and found Tanner's aura surrounding his hands. It was a deep blue around the edges and grew lighter the closer to his skin. Her own aura was the opposite, only in purple. It was darker at her skin and got lighter to the edges.

Focusing on her aura, she tried to define the colors within and separate them. That proved harder than it sounded. Before she could get totally frustrated, she slowed her breathing and searched for the two colors that made purple.

Finding the red and blue strains, she moved the red away until her aura was blue. Good. Now she had to move the darker color to the outside of her energy bubble. She did that by taking hold of the white string and pulling it closer to her. Relief flowed over her when it worked and her aura matched Tanner's.

Now what? Oh, yeah. She had to bring the energy to her. Slowly she pulled her hands toward her body while directing her aura into her.

Like a dull light suddenly filling a dark room, her

mind formed a barrier. It was thin, but a hell of a lot more than she had before.

Holding the thin wall around her mind, she held her hand up in front of her face, palms facing Tanner. "Slowly press your palms to mine."

In slow movements, he lifted his hands and inched them closer to hers. He touched his fingertips to hers and waited. A spark of worry tingled through her hands. When she smiled and nodded to him to continue, he pressed his hands to hers.

She shuddered at the contact, but for a brief moment, she picked up on only a slight transfer of a memory. Then her thin shield crashed, letting in a wave of images. She jerked her hands away from Tanner and slapped them to the rock floor. The images faded just as quickly as they appeared, and she smiled.

"That was great. Let's do it again."

****

"What the fuck is going on?"

Keegan's voice echoed off the cave walls as he stood inside the doorway, his gaze fixed on the two sentries sitting on the floor way too close to Addyson.

The four of them stood and faced him, and the males—including Will—moved to stand protectively in front of her. Did they really think he'd hurt her?

Keegan's leopard growled inside his head, seeing the males as a threat to someone who belonged to him, to his mate.

"Answer the damned question," he growled.

Addyson stepped forward, but the sentries moved to block her. Keegan growled again. The sight of the other males blocking her from him only pissed him off more.

Mine.

Tanner tensed, his muscles flexing as though he was preparing himself for a fight. "We were helping her build her shields."

Keegan took a step closer, ignoring the wolf. Nor did he care what Tanner had to say. A possessive need filled him, and all he wanted at that moment was Addyson. With his eyes trained on her, he watched as she darted from behind the sentries to come around to stand between Keegan and them.

She laid a hand on his chest, halting him. "They were helping me. Will, too. I created a shield and, with practice, can make it stronger."

He peered down at her. She smiled weakly as if unsure. He frowned and studied her for several moments before what she said sank in. Shields?

Fuck.

She was trying to rebuild the natural shields that kept her gift in check.

Keegan moved his gaze to Will, who stood apart from the others, wringing his hands and looking as though he was about to bolt at any minute.

"Out," he commanded.

Tanner and Kirk hesitated, but at Addyson's nod, they walked out of the cave. Keegan knew they didn't go far. He could hear them shuffling about a few yards from the entrance.

"Sir?"

Keegan snapped his gaze to Will, who now stood next to them with his head held high. Keegan breathed in deeply through his nose then exhaled slowly while he tried to keep from physically moving the teen out of his way. "Will, go with the sentries."

The boy turned to peer at Addyson. "Will you be

okay?"

She smiled and nodded. Will slowly made his way to the entrance of the cave.

Once the stone door slid into place, Keegan closed the very short distance between them. She didn't move, nor did she flinch when he snaked an arm around her waist and drew her into his body, hard. A soft gasp escaped her, and she rested her palms on his chest.

Even through the cotton of the tee he wore, he felt the growing heat that was always there between them.

He peered into her violet eyes and frowned. There was a hint of fear hiding behind the strength and control she clung to, although he wasn't sure if the fear was of him or something else.

"Are you going to stare at me all night?" she said as she lifted her chin a little higher.

He felt the right corner of his mouth twitch. "Are you always so brave?"

She swallowed, and flecks of lavender rippled through her irises. "Only with you," she whispered then looked away.

He hooked a finger under her chin and lifted her gaze back to his. "Why is that?" He suspected the answer but wanted to hear it from her.

"You're the only one I can have skin-to-skin contact with and not suffer for it."

"No pain at all?" he asked while he searched her face. He couldn't penetrate her mind to see if she was being truthful. It wasn't that he didn't believe her, but he wouldn't put it past Addyson to leave out certain details so he wouldn't worry about her.

She drew her brows together, causing creases to form on her forehead. Keegan fought the urge to kiss them away. When she focused on his face, not quite making eye contact, she said, "No, none at all. It's like everything is...quiet? Maybe my mind is more broken than I thought."

She pushed against him to try to break his hold as if she wanted to step away. He let her go and was relieved when she didn't put more than a foot between them. "Your mind is not broken." When she opened her mouth as if to argue, he held up a hand. "When I'm touching you, the hum inside my head goes away."

She blinked then drew her eyebrows together. "What about your telepathy?"

He raised his hand to touch her cheek, but she took a step back. That made his leopard growl and claw inside him. "It doesn't work." It came out a little rougher than he intended, but Addyson didn't flinch.

"Not at all?"

He shrugged and turned to survey the room. The sofa was pushed back a couple of feet, no doubt to make room for Addyson, Will, and the sentries to sit on the floor. However, Keegan thought he liked the couch where it was. It made the living area appear bigger.

His heart ached and made his chest feel tight. Why had he come here of all places? Because it was the safest place for Addyson and Will.

He heard Addyson's bare feet shuffle over the stone floor, and he closed his eyes. Her scent was too enticing, too much. He didn't know how much longer he'd be able to keep the control over the throbbing need in his pants.

"What is this place?"

He turned to face her again and narrowed his eyes. Her tone told him she already knew, or at least knew some of it.

Damn Pack rumor mill.

"I found this cave about six months before Cate became pregnant with our third child. I was hunting and stumbled upon it. We'd come here during hunts when we wanted to get away from the others for a moment or two. When she found out she was pregnant, I worked on it as much as I could in secret. I wanted it to be a surprise." He paused to take a deep breath and push back the building fury and pain. Too much of what he'd learned over the last few days had brought back the pain of betrayal. The knowledge his daughter had been alive all this time and living in the Onyx den only built up the fury more. Yes, he was happy to know she was alive, but at the same time worried about whose side she'd turn to when she found out.

And she'd find out. Keegan would make sure of it.

He peered into Addyson's gaze and continued. "It was going to be a safe place for her to deliver the baby and stay until she was strong enough to return to the den. The war with Onyx had us both worried."

Addyson nodded and stepped closer. "What happened?"

He shook his head and started to pace. "I can't, Addy. Not now." Coming to a stop in front of her, he cursed himself when he saw the disappointment in her face. He reached for her and was relieved when she didn't pull away from him. He took her hand and brought it to place over his heart. "I'll tell you someday soon."

She lifted her violet gaze to his and nodded. "I trust you."

He smiled but whispered, "I'm not so sure I trust myself, especially when comes to being alone with you."

Then he released her hand and turned to head outside to find Tanner.

CHAPTER FIVE

Addyson let out a breath and sat down on the sofa. Her whole body trembled, but not from fear. She was on the verge of sensory overload. Sure, she didn't suffer pain or have crippling visions at his touch, but it'd been far too long since she'd been able to rely on a Pack mate for the comfort of skin-to-skin contact.

Her leopard was touch-starved to the extreme, and the more Keegan offered, the more she fought for control over her cat.

Shifters needed the simple touches from Pack members just as much as they needed the air they breathed. The only way she was able to keep from going completing insane was Keegan. He was the only one she could have minimal contact with.

And he knew it.

He'd also been trying to drive her over the edge in the last couple of weeks. That was why she needed to learn to build her shields and strengthen her resistance toward the male.

A smile lifted her lips, and she leaned back on the couch. Pride filled her chest. She'd built the first layer of her mental shield by using Tanner's aura. However, it was a very weak layer.

She didn't need to think too hard on why Keegan could break through her shields. It had nothing to do with his telepathic abilities. He'd confirmed that when he admitted he couldn't read her and she was a haven of sorts for him.

No, Keegan Andrews was her mate.

She'd known this from the first time she'd met him, but his heart still belonged to a ghost.

With a groan, Addyson pushed herself to a stand and went to the kitchen to start dinner. She really needed to get a grip and shove her schoolgirl fantasy of Keegan and mating out of her mind, no matter how much it hurt.

She reached the kitchen just as the stone door slid open and Keegan walked in with his youngest son, Alec, and Luna's middle son, Dane, following behind. She smiled and nodded at the enforcers. "Are you two staying for dinner?"

Alec gave her a crooked grin. "Sure. I'd never turn down a meal."

Keegan growled low in his throat. "Addyson is working on building her shields, so she won't be wearing her gloves. As long as you are careful you may stay."

Addyson ignored Keegan's grumpy tone and asked, "Any special request?"

Dane, carrying a black case, stepped forward to stand even with Alec. "Anything for me is good." He turned to

Keegan and asked, "Where do you want this set up?"

Keegan pointed to a desk along the far wall. "Over there."

The wolf Beta nodded and proceeded to the desk, set the case on it, and opened it to reveal a laptop and other equipment Addyson didn't recognize.

"What is that?" she asked as she watched Dane pull out cables and a small black box.

"It's our security system and a secure way to communicate with the Pack," Keegan replied in a matter-of-fact tone.

Addyson pursed her lips and started pulling things out of the fridge. She really didn't know what the sudden shift in Keegan's mood was all about, but as soon as they were alone, she'd find out.

Will climbed up on a stool on the other side of the counter. She offered him a smile then studied him for a few moments. A thought came to mind, and she couldn't believe she hadn't asked him before. "Are there others? Scribes, I mean. What about your family?"

Will looked away from her to watch Alec and Dane work on the security system while they talked to Keegan. "I'm not sure. I've never heard anyone mention it inside Onyx. As for my family, my whole den was destroyed."

Addyson's heart broke for the boy. She reached over the counter and covered his hand and squeezed. "Oh, hun, I'm so sorry."

He shrugged. "They live in my heart. When I'm stronger, I'm going to ask Blaine if I can join the next round of soldier training. I'm going to fight in the war."

Keegan walked over then and sat on the stool next to Will. "I think you'll make a good soldier."

Will sat a little straighter and smiled. "I want to help bring Onyx down."

Addyson met Keegan's gaze for a moment before

bending to put the roast in the oven. She heard the pride in Keegan's voice as he said, "You'll get your chance one day. We'll all get our chance."

****

Keegan stepped out of the cave and found Alec, in leopard form, stretched out on a large branch in the nearby oak tree. Keegan knew his son wasn't sleeping. The male was too calculating and lethal to let his guard down. Alec might be the leopard Beta until Blaine announced otherwise, but Keegan's youngest son held the power of an alpha.

Alec flicked his tail in a sign that he knew Keegan was there. Keegan sent his son a thought. "I'm meeting Kieran. I shouldn't be gone long."

"She'll be fine. Dane is running a perimeter check."

Keegan nodded and started off toward the west to a neutral part of the mountain that had been left unclaimed by the Packs in the Smoky Mountain/Blue Ridge Mountain region. There were only a handful of neutral areas now thanks to Onyx and their bastard mutants.

He stopped at a small stream about a half-mile from the cave where he'd left Addyson sleeping, peered into the water as it rushed by, and waited. Kieran was never on time. Not that Keegan blamed him. The male was a spy after all.

The crunching of leaves under heavy footfalls made Keegan glance over his shoulder. Kieran leaned against a tree several feet away, his large arms folded over his chest. Keegan turned and sat on a boulder. "You look well."

One of Kieran's shoulders raised in a half-hearted shrug. "I manage."

Kieran had once been the Marshal of Ashwood before Blaine came of age to claim the title and the Pack had almost been completely destroyed by the rogues. By all rights, Kieran should be serving on the Council of the Elders, but that too was gone. Very few elders existed, and those who had survived lived in hiding. Many were hidden away by their Packs because they were the Pack's only link to the past and the history that was passed down from generation to generation.

So Kieran had mentored Blaine into his role of Marshal and then taken a seat as a senior enforcer until the day he left and the Pack believed he had gone rogue. Keegan didn't do anything to discredit the rumor. No, he let the rumor circulate and reach their enemy's ears. Besides, it made it easier for Kieran to find a place inside the Onyx den.

Keegan narrowed his eyes and demanded, "Show me the proof."

Kieran casually reached inside his jacket pocket, pulled out something, and tossed it over to Keegan. He caught it in midair. When he opened his palm, his heart stopped. "Where the fuck did you get this?"

Fury built up inside him as he stared down at the rose-shaped locket he'd given Cate on their first date. She had said she lost it while on a run. She'd cried for hours over the damn thing.

This had to be some kind of a sick joke, Onyx's attempt of hurting him from the grave.

"From Ana."

Keegan snapped his head up and met the other male's gaze. "Who?"

Kieran nodded to the locket. "Open it."

Keegan opened the locket. At first his brain refused

to recognize what he was seeing. After a few moments he saw the woman who looked too much like Cate to be anyone but her daughter. "Her name is Ana?"

"Zorana, but she likes to be called Ana."

Zorana. That was the name Cate had picked out, saying it was exotic and beautiful, just like their little girl would be.

Keegan didn't miss the subtle note of compassion in Kieran's tone. Keegan studied the male before saying, "She's your mate."

Kieran took a deep breath and unfolded his arms. "I haven't claimed her. I can't. Felix has raised her as his daughter and forbids anyone from mating her or touching her." A tic formed in Kieran's temples as if the idea pissed him off as much as it did Keegan. "Felix would kill her and drop her off at your doorstep, if he knew you even suspected she was alive."

Keegan rolled his fingers around the locket and stood to pace. "Why are you telling me now?"

Kieran ran a hand through his dark hair. "Because I need to get her out of the den. I think Felix has caught on to the fact that I'm a spy, or at least he's starting to believe I might be. His new Marshal is a nosy son of a bitch and has a big mouth. I'm not sure how much either of them knows. There is also a small group in the Pack that plans to break away and join a small shifter rebel group."

Rebels? Fuck. What's next?

Keegan started to pace again. "Okay, we need a plan. You have to stay in and rebut the rumors. Do what you must to keep Felix from finding out the truth for a little while longer."

"What are you going to do?"

"I'm not sure." Keegan turned away to head back to the cave but stopped and looked over his shoulder. "Tell

Felix that Ashwood Falls has a new leopard Alpha."

Kieran lips twitched. "You're hoping he goes after you directly now?"

Keegan didn't answer. He didn't have to. Kieran knew him too well, and he also knew the laws. Alphas couldn't directly attack one another.

Even though the Onyx Pack had broken just about every peace law set in place, Felix hadn't broken the Alpha rule and come after Keegan. It seemed the rogue leader had learned his lesson from before.

Felix hadn't gone after only Keegan; he'd gone after Luna as well. Hitting both Pack Alphas had made the two Packs band together as one Pack and fight to bring down Onyx once and for all.

Now that Keegan wasn't Alpha, he was free to track the rogue Alpha down.

Just like Felix was able to hunt him.

CHAPTER SIX

Addyson dried her hands and laid the kitchen towel on the counter. She was itching for something to do. Her cat paced under her skin wanting out, but she couldn't run like she wanted and needed. She was in unfamiliar territory where rogues could track her down.

No. They couldn't track her anymore.

She lifted her hand to the base of her neck, feeling the small scar. Beneath it had once been a GPS tracking device Felix had order to be implanted soon after she was abducted. She'd woken in Ashwood's medical center scared that she'd endangered the Pack until Danica, the leopard Healer, told her that the tracking device had been removed and destroyed.

She froze as she thought about the GPS and went in search of Will. She found him in the room he'd chosen, stretched out on the bed reading on the e-reader that Keegan had given him. Will looked up and met her eyes.

"Is something wrong?" he asked, concern etched into his face.

Addyson walked farther into the room and whispered, "Do you have a tracker in your skin?"

He smiled as though he'd been caught stealing milk from a kitten and turned to show her the back of his neck. She sat down on the bed beside him and reached out to trace the small scar. "When did you remove it?"

He turned to face her and shrugged. "The night I ran from Onyx."

"But they tracked you to the den."

"Because I was too slow," he said, disgust in his tone. "Someone opened my cell door. I hesitated. I guess I thought it was a trick."

Addyson frowned. "Someone let you go?"

Will nodded. "Yes. They wore gloves, so I couldn't get any feedback from the lock."

They fell silent for a moment. Addyson remembered hearing Keegan talk about Graham's kidnapping and how someone had unlocked his cell as well. She studied Will again. "I don't understand."

Will turned off his e-reader and set it on the bed beside him. "Some Onyx members are planning to break from the Pack."

"How do you know that?"

Keegan's voice made them both jump. Addyson scrambled off the bed to stand in front of Will, blocking him from the Alpha. Keegan raised a brow. "I'm not going to hurt him, Addy."

Her heart quickened at the nickname he'd given her, the one he used to calm her when she was afraid and started to freak out.

She folded her arms over her chest and glared. "I

take it you already knew about the rebel rogues."

Keegan's lips twitched. "I just found out. Will, answer the question."

Will got off the bed to stand next to Addyson. "I picked up small objects when they let me out of my cell. A few of them held memories and conversations about breaking away from the Pack."

Keegan's stern look softened, and he nodded. "You don't happen to have the names of these rebels, do you?"

Will smiled back at the Alpha and said, "Only one. Sable. She's leading the group."

Keegan's brows dipped. "Are you sure?"

Will nodded, and Addyson shook her head at the same time. "She's Felix's daughter and the Beta of the Pack. Why would she go against him?"

"I'm not sure, but I don't think it's out of the good of her heart." Keegan growled. Addyson couldn't have agreed more. She'd witnessed Sable's ruthless leadership.

After a short silence, Keegan said, "You need a run."

She snapped her gaze to his at the command in his tone. Her very short fuse just got shorter. "Is that an order?"

One corner of his sensual mouth lifted, and damn it if she didn't melt a little. He held his hand out to her and softened his expression. "Come running with me."

She shook her head, trying like hell to not be effected by the male in front of her. "I'm fine," she lied and moved to walk around him. She needed some air, without Keegan around. She needed to be alone to think.

The truth was that she didn't know how to handle the male. He was too much and everywhere she turned.

"Addyson."

Her name on his lips gave her pause. He spoke it on

a purr as he followed her to the living room, and damn if she didn't want to kiss those lips. But what would that do to her? Would it finally break her to have so much skin contact with the male who ignited the flame within her?

Oh, God. He was too much male right now.

She turned toward the door and slid the stone slab aside. She bolted through the opening, not paying attention to what, or who, might be in front of her and ran right into a solid mass. Instinctually she reached out and made skin-to-skin contact with Blaine, Keegan's eldest son and the new leopard Alpha of Ashwood Falls.

Images slammed into her mind's eye, taking her to the place Blaine had been in this particular vision. He was running through the forest, panic raging through his veins. Every breath, every step, and every thought he had at the time was now hers. It always happened like that. Without her shields, her mind was open to everything the person felt, saw, smelt, and tasted.

She jerked back from Blaine, only to have her knees give out. Tears streamed down her cheeks as she crumbled to the ground. The vision didn't stop because she broke the contact with Blaine. No it played on like a horror movie she was unable to turn off.

She barely heard Keegan's feral growl, warning everyone to stay away from her.

Her head ached, and she tried desperately to control the speed of the vision and push away the harsh, painful emotions that felt too real to not be hers.

The vision was a mess of images, and she couldn't make sense of it. Flashes of Keegan's face, marred with anger and horror, then a glimpse of a brunette woman with tears in her eyes and a gun raised to her temple.

She felt arms come around her and lift her then the scent of oak and spice filled her senses. Keegan. She inhaled deeply. The pain eased as she felt him move with her cradled to his chest.

The images slowed, finally. Before the flood shut off, she realized that the woman was Keegan's mate. Oh, God, Blaine had watched his mother kill herself.

She wasn't sure how long Keegan held her in silence, but she allowed herself to drink up the masculine heat of him. It soothed her and her cat in a way nothing had ever done.

And she knew why. She'd always known.

Whether she wanted to admit it or not, Keegan was her mate. Her own protectiveness rose to the surface as the vision replayed in her mind, this time without the heavy, heart-crushing emotions.

The visions were always like that. The initial impact slammed into her with so much force it left her a quaking mess on the floor. She hated that anyone had to see her like that, hated that her mind was broken.

Before she was captured by Onyx and forced to use her powers until she wasn't able to shield from them any longer, she'd had a mental wall in place that blocked out the psychic impressions from others. The constant use of that power overloaded her senses.

Felix Darwin got off on her pain as he thirsted for more information on Ashwood and their allies. Never allowing her the much-needed rest between visions, he forced her to touch objects over and over until she was no longer able to block anything or anyone from her powers.

If she refused, which she did often, Felix found creative ways to punish her.

She shuddered and let out a soft whimper. Her cat curled up in a ball and shook inside her. Keegan's arms tightened around her, bringing her back to the present.

As much as she wanted to wrap her arms around

this male and relish the peace he seemed to give her, she wasn't naïve enough to believe he was offering anything more than an Alpha would for any one of his submissives when they needed him. She pulled back, only to have him draw her closer into his body.

Her leopard whined.

Keegan dipped his fingers into her hair and massaged her scalp. She groaned at the intimate caress and gave into the need to be cared for by this male, even if it meant she was sending her heart false hope.

After a few more moments of silence, Addyson took a shaky breath and wiped her tear-soaked cheeks. "Where is everyone?"

Keegan wiped hair from her forehead. "Outside."

She sagged in relief. It was bad enough for Keegan to see her this way. She didn't need, nor want, an audience. She also didn't want to move from her very comfortable spot where her head rested on Keegan's chest. The thump, thump of his steady heartbeat soothed her.

Too bad he had his shirt on...

Squashing that thought, she focused back on the vision and drummed up the courage to tell Keegan what she'd seen.

"I saw your mate," she rushed out and didn't move while she waited for his reaction.

He tensed under her, and she felt a tinge of pain spark from him. She wasn't empathic, not really. She felt others emotions through touch and she could sense others' feelings by just being around them. However, she couldn't influence emotions like a true empath. Yet she could see through the wall Keegan hid behind. She could see his pain. She could also see that he was on the path to healing that wound.

Addyson so wanted to help him move forward. She didn't care how long it took, she'd help him and wait for him. He was her mate after all.

"What do you mean?"

She swallowed hard. "I saw how she died."

****

Fuck, fuck, and fuck!

Keegan gently eased Addyson off his lap and stood to pace the living room. His heart pounded inside his chest as the buried pain surfaced, putting his leopard on alert. A whirlwind of thoughts and questions invaded his mind, the number one being how Blaine would have known about his mother's suicide.

Sparing a glance at Addyson over his shoulder, he cursed again. Her red-rimmed eyes and tear-streaked cheeks didn't hide her compassion and concern.

Damn it, she'd felt his pain. Or was it Blaine's?

Hell, whichever the case, she now knew the truth. Apparently Blaine did, too, but Keegan would deal with his son later. Right now he had to face the past with the woman of his future.

Talk about ripping off the bandage off.

"What did you see?"

Addyson wiped her eyes and sat straighter on the sofa then smoothed out the hem of her lavender top against her jeans. Keegan forced himself to be patient with her. She was a submissive after all. If he pushed, her cat would make her bare her neck and submit totally to him.

He didn't want that. He wanted the woman who possessed a fire within her that he guessed no one had seen but him.

So he waited. When she did speak, she lifted her gaze

to his. "I saw the two of you through Blaine's eyes. You and Cate were arguing. No, not arguing." She swallowed again and averted his gaze as she whispered the next sentence. "You were pleading with her to come home."

He closed his eyes. It was the nightmare he'd had since that night. "She'd been feeding information to Felix for years. One of my soldiers told me they smelt a rogue on her. I didn't want to believe it, but something gnawed at me to find out. So I waited for her to return from her evening walk."

Addyson lifted her gaze back up to his, waiting for him to finish. Keegan ran a hand through his hair. "She was upset, as if she'd just had an argument with someone. Felix's scent was all over her."

Addyson gasped and quietly asked, "What did you do?"

He sighed and sat down in the chair across from her. "I was so angry, and the thought of another male's scent on her, my enemy at that, made me lose control over my leopard. It's all a blur really. I confronted her about his scent and what the soldier said. I'd just come off patrol and still had my gun in my chest holster. In my rage, I didn't expect Cate to reach out and take it. She ran into the forest, away from the den."

Addyson nodded as if piecing the rest of it together. "Blaine must had heard or felt the distress and followed. He found you begging her to return home, but she said she'd betrayed the Pack and..."

She cut off her own statement with a sob. "Oh, Keegan. I didn't mean to. I didn't know..."

He crossed the small space between them and cupped her face in his hands. "You did nothing wrong. I was the one who pushed you when I knew that you'd run from me. I knew Blaine was at the door but didn't think I'd frightened you enough to run outside."

She stilled and stared into his eyes. The male in front of her made her feel things she hadn't in a very long time. Things she'd didn't remember feeling, ever. "You don't scare me. You're dominance does. I'm not sure how to react around you, to your leopard. If I'm to touch you, to comfort you. Especially since you're my mate."

His chest tightened as he peered into her violet eyes and let her words settle in his mind. She was his mate. He'd known that from the moment he found her in the forest. Yet to hear the words on her tongue made something inside him tighten and his leopard purr. Not wanting to think about anything else, he leaned in and brushed his lips against hers.

She gasped as their lips touched, but didn't draw away. He took that as an invitation and hardened the kiss, sliding his tongue inside her mouth. Her tongue tangled with his, intensifying the need rushing through him.

Keegan slid one hand down her back then slipped it under her shirt. When his fingers touched her bare skin, he heard her sharp intake of breath. He also sensed the colliding emotions of fear, desire, and confusion building inside her.

Breaking the kiss, he drew back and peered into her gaze. "Are you okay?"

She looked down at her hands pressed against his chest and shook her head. "It's too much. The touching. It's too much right now."

He nipped at her nose, drawing a smile from her. "Then I'll have to make sure to desensitize you."

She looked back up, her eyes grew round, and he heard her pulse kick up a couple of beats per second. "How?"

It came out barely a whisper, but he heard it. "By touching you and playing with you more."

"Oh." She looked around, as if searching the room for something, or someone.

With his finger under her chin, he gently urged her to meet his stare. "You're right. We are mates, and you're mine to keep and play with."

He stood and took her hand. "I'll draw you a bath so you can relax while I talk to my son."

CHAPTER SEVEN

Addyson eased down into the bath and sighed as the warm water flowed over her too-sensitive skin. She sank down under the water until it touched her chin, and she closed her eyes.

...and you're mine to keep and play with.

Keegan's words drifted through her mind. There was a promise and a demand in those words. She was old enough to know that once an Alpha saw something he wanted, he got it.

Well, hell, Addy, you had to go and challenge him.

That's exactly what she'd done when she confessed she knew they were mates. And he answered. That was something she hadn't expected, especially with the subject of his dead mate hanging between them.

Then there was that kiss. Never in her life had she been so turned on. Her skin felt as though it were on fire where his fingers touched. It was all too much, sending her senses into overdrive. She'd lost the ability to breathe for a moment, and it scared the hell out her.

Flashes of the Onyx soldiers touching her overwhelmed her and stole the pleasure she'd felt with Keegan.

Taking a deep breath, she pushed the ugly, evil thoughts out of her mind. She'd lived too long with the ugliness, and she refused to let it cloud her now.

It appeared that Keegan was her future, and she wasn't going to let Onyx win at destroying what little happiness she could have. Her happiness lay in Ashwood with Keegan.

As long as she could figure out away to help him heal.

With a purpose, she bathed, dried off, dressed, and headed to the living room, where the males were in a heated discussion. Most likely about her vision.

Addyson entered the living room on silent bare feet, but Keegan knew the moment she entered the room. He stopped speaking and turned to her. Addyson fought off a gasp at the intensity in his gaze. His brown eyes held swirls of gold, indicating his leopard wasn't far from the surface.

She took an involuntary step back, making him turn his body to face her. When he started to walk toward her, she froze. Her leopard whimpered in her head, but the woman held his gaze. Normally, submissives didn't look their dominants in the eyes as they were being stalked. It was a sign of aggression and the dominant would see it as a challenge.

However, Addyson knew deep down that Keegan could never hurt her. As his mate, she needed to be strong and show him she wouldn't back down from him.

And she wouldn't run. Not from him. Not ever again.

He stopped inches from her. His lips twitched as he slowly brought his hand up to stroke her cheek. All the tension fled her body, and she leaned into his touch.

"How was your bath?" he whispered.

She smiled. "It was nice." She rose up on her toes and kissed his cheek then walked around him to greet Blaine. "How are your mates and the kids?"

The stern glare he had when she'd first come into the room softened. "They're wonderful."

She stepped closer and concentrated on blocking his psychic energy. Like with Tanner, she used Blaine's aura to create a mental shield surrounding her mind. She offered Blaine her hand. She heard Keegan step up behind her, but he didn't touch her, just growled out, "What are you doing?"

"I need to practice building my shields," she replied in a firm tone that made her want to apologize, but Blaine shook his head as if telling her to stay strong.

Blaine sat up on the sofa and hovered his hand over hers then looked her in the eyes. She could only hold his stare for a second before peering down at their hands. "Are you sure about this, Addyson?"

She nodded. "I won't see the same vision twice. I've been working on rebuilding my shields."

Hesitantly, he placed his hand on hers. His Alpha power washed over her in a soothing caress. It felt familiar and like home.

She didn't get hit with a vision from the connection. She relaxed and almost became giddy at how easy it was getting to block others the more she did it.

Then a blurred image of two males, bodies entwined together in a bed, came into her mind's eye. She gasped and jerked her hand back, her cheeks heating.

"Addyson?" Blaine and Keegan asked at the same

time.

She waved them off and shook her head. "I'm fine. It was a...happy vision and fuzzy."

Keegan wrapped his fingers around the back of her neck and massaged her tense muscles. "That's good, right?"

She leaned her back into him. "Yes. It seems when I try to shield I pull the most recent happy event."

Blaine cleared his throat and met her gaze. Addyson held in a smile but quickly averted her eyes, her submissive nature not allowing her to hold his stare for more than a few moments.

Keegan kissed the top of her head and nudged her to sit. Automatically she went to take a step toward the sofa then stopped. She turned to Blaine then Alec, lodged in an armchair to their left and Will silently sitting on the sofa next to Blaine. "Would you like tea or coffee?"

They nodded, and she turned to the kitchen where she filled the kettle with water and placed it on the stove. A few moments later, Will entered and came over to stand next to her as she filled the tray with cups and the fixings for tea and coffee.

Will reached out and touched her arm. "Are you okay?"

She stopped and turned to him, brushing his too-long hair out of his eyes. "Yes. The bath Keegan drew for me helped."

She caught a shy grin before he looked away, most likely trying to hide it from her. "He likes you," he whispered.

She sighed. "I know." It was all she could say right now. There were too many uncertainties between them. The pain too sharp, their pasts haunting them both.

She tried to replay the vision over in her mind again. Something about it didn't sit well with her. A mate just didn't betray the other, not under their own power anyway. Addyson was almost tempted to go back out there and take Blaine's hand in an attempt to bring back the vision.

She couldn't do that. It had nearly broken her all over again the first time. The small shield she'd created wasn't strong enough. Not yet.

Determination drove her to do whatever it would take to strengthen those shields so she could become the woman she once was. Well, at least as strong as she used to be, if not stronger.

"Do you think she was controlled?" Alec's voice drifted from the living room. He spoke loud enough that his voice echoed off the stone walls of the cave.

Most likely to be heard over Keegan's and Blaine's heated discussion of Cate.

Addyson closed her eyes. She wished they'd stop arguing so she could think. Then Alec's question settled into her thoughts and she stilled. Controlled? Damn. That was it. She turned to Will and asked him to bring the tea and coffee in when the kettle sounded. He nodded, but she felt his concerned gaze on her as she left the kitchen.

Keegan and Blaine stared at Alec as though they expected him to grow a new limb or something.

"I believe she had been," she blurted

They turned their gazes to her now. Keegan started to shake his head. "It's not possible."

Addyson didn't take her gaze from him as she disagreed. "It is, and I saw Felix do it more times than I like to remember."

Keegan turned his body to face her and started stalking toward her. She forced her legs not to shake and her body to stay planted in place. The tension in the air coming from Keegan made it hard not to revert to her submissive nature.

He stopped a few inches from her, the heat of his body caressing her still too-sensitive skin. Yet, she didn't break eye contact as she reached out and placed her palm on his chest. He closed his eyes for several moments, and when he opened them, she saw a hint of gratitude.

"It wasn't her fault," she whispered.

Keegan stroked his fingers down her cheek then stepped back, the pain too raw in his gaze. He was too stubborn, too fixed on burying the pain to see the logic behind what she'd just told him. It frustrated her and made her heart ache for him all at once.

Without another word, Keegan turned to the door and left. She took a step but stopped when Blaine said, "Let him go. He needs to run off the frustration and think."

She dropped her shoulders but nodded. Blaine was right. Keegan needed time to think and run off the building emotions. She couldn't imagine what he was feeling after what he'd learned over the last few days.

She'd give him time to think, for now. He needed to talk about it, figure out where to go from here. And she was going to see that he did.

CHAPTER EIGHT

Keegan stepped out into the cooling evening air, unable to draw enough of it into his lungs. His head spun with the possibilities surrounding Cate's death. Could Felix have controlled her, forced her to betray Keegan and the Pack? He wanted so desperately to believe it because, in his heart, he knew she'd never willingly betray her family. And Pack was family.

Yet, there was a small part of him that doubted the possibility of a mindbender. They were rare. The few times Keegan had come face-to-face with Felix, he'd never sensed the ability in the rogue Alpha. There was only one way Keegan wouldn't have detected the other male's power.

It would have to mean that Felix had dual psychic abilities.

Another impossibility.

Or was it?

Keegan took off through the thick trees surrounding the cave. He didn't shift because his human side needed to run more than the leopard, although he did allow the cat to come to the surface and enjoy the run just as much.

He came to a stop at a small stream and scented the air. A low growl rumbled up his chest to his throat. The unmistakable stench of the mutants Onyx used as their assassins drifted in the wind. The hairs on the back of Keegan's neck stood on end, and his whole body went taut with tension.

Damn bastards will not take another mate from me.

Keegan's leopard roared in agreement and paced beneath his skin.

The shuffling of footsteps had him whirling around to come face-to-face with a large wolf mutant. The half-man, half-wolf stood over seven feet tall with fangs that jetted out of his top jaw to stretch over his bottom lip.

When Keegan shifted one hand into a claw and allowed his own fangs to release from his gums, he sensed another presence come up on his right.

"I wouldn't challenge that one, Alpha. Or should I say Elder?"

Keegan turned to the unfamiliar voice while keeping the mutant in his line of sight. Narrowing his eyes, Keegan sent out his senses to the male and hit a mental wall. The bastard was either naturally resistant to Keegan's telepathy or he'd development the ability to block it. "Who are you?

The male smirked. "The name is Van. I hold his leash," he indicated the mutant next to him, "and those of others like him. I'm also the new Marshal of Onyx."

Keegan ground his molars and breathed in through

his nose slowly. The half-ass meditating routine didn't help soothe his already pissed-off mood. "That tells me nothing."

The male shrugged. Arrogance rolled off him, thick and oily. His dark hair was cut short to the scalp, and his midnight-blue eyes held a darkness Keegan had seen before. Felix possessed the same evil within him.

Van locked gazes with Keegan then grinned to show the tips of his fangs. "I know you know about your daughter and your plan to steal her away from her pack. Soon Felix will too."

Fear burned inside Keegan's gut. There was no telling what Felix would do to Ana just to send a message to Keegan.

Not happening. Keegan had to trust that Kieran would keep her safe until they came up with a solid plan to get her out.

Van laughed. The evil sound sent a cold shiver up Keegan's spine. "She is very pretty and strong. I bet she'd give some male lots of sons."

Fury boiled in Keegan's veins, and he charged forward, aiming straight at Van's throat, only to be knocked to the ground right before his teeth made contact. He slid along the ground and slammed into a tree. Pain raced up his spine, as the breath was knocked out of him.

Shaking off the pain, Keegan rushed the mutant, nailing him in the gut and taking him to the ground. Keegan struck out with his clawed hand and scratched the beast down the side of its long snout. Blood oozed from the wounds, and the mutant yelled out in fury and pain.

Keegan hit him again, harder. Much too fast, the mutant's hand came up and gripped Keegan's throat, cutting off his airway. The mutant rolled them over so he straddled Keegan and raised his clawed fist over Keegan's heart.

Keegan braced for impact, knowing good and well that in this position he was done for. Mutants' brains were too jumbled, their thought patterns too wild. That was one of the reason the Onyx Pack used them to fight against Ashwood Falls.

Keegan reached in with his telepathy to distract the creature long enough to break free.

In the next moment, the mutant froze in place. Confusion followed by pain crossed his face before he looked down at the point of a blade sticking out of his chest. His body jerked, and then he fell to the ground. In his place stood a woman with long raven hair.

His heart stopped for a few moments before it jolted back to life, hammering against his ribcage.

Cate.

It was the only thought he had as he peered into the gray eyes—Cate's eyes. They were the same color as Blaine's.

By the way she stood over him frozen in place she was as shocked as he was. Then her eyebrows drew together, and she pulled another dagger from a sheath strapped to her thigh and raised it at him. "Who are you?"

Keegan laid his head on the ground and looked at the darkening sky. "Keegan Andrews, Elder of Ashwood Falls."

She pursed her lips and said, "I thought there weren't any more Elders."

"I'm a new breed," he said dryly as he rolled to a sitting position.

Ana tensed and shook the dagger toward him. "Stay where you are."

He met her eyes. She stared back with the strength

of a dominant female facing a challenge. A challenge she'd be glad to take on, he bet. Keegan smirked. His daughter held the strength of an alpha.

He eased to a stand, forcing Ana to shift uneasily from foot to foot. Facing her, he held up his hands because he didn't want to spook her and end up with that dagger buried in chest. "Thank you for saving my life."

Her gaze flicked to the dead mutant beside them, and then back to him. "I hate the mutants. Vile beasts."

He grinned, turned his back to her, and walked off. His grin turned into a chuckle as he heard her curse and start to follow him. "I said stay put."

He twisted around and came nose to nose with her. With quick efficiency, he disarmed her of the dagger and threw the thing into a large oak about ten feet away.

"Hey!" She glared at him as if ordering him to retrieve her knife.

Not happening.

Without realizing what he was doing, he reached out to touch her face. She recoiled and stepped back. He pushed away the ache in his chest from the rejection. She didn't know him, didn't know he was her father.

Leaning into her, he whispered, "I owe you a debt for my life, but I can't pay it today."

She stilled. "What kind of debt?"

He stepped back because it was too tempting to grab her and take her to the den, lock her up until she knew the truth and accepted it. No, he couldn't do that. That was what Felix had done, except the bastard had stolen her and built her a life on lies.

"You saved my life. So anything you need just ask." He turned again to head toward the cave.

He got about twenty feet away when she asked, "How will I find you?"

Without looking at her, he said, "Ask Kieran." Then he darted off into the woods faster than he knew she'd be able to follow. Not many could track him. His son-in-law and the Pack Tracker, Travis, had difficulties following his trail.

No, there was only one who wasn't bound to him that could track him.

That male currently lived inside the Onyx den, and his scent was all over Ana.

Keegan hoped Ana trusted Kieran enough to tell him about the meeting and that she'd soon come to collect on the debt Keegan owed her.

****

The only thing Addyson didn't like about her new temporary home was the lack of windows. So she'd come outside to sit in the grass next to the door. The wolf Marshal, Hayden, growled at her when she tried to wander beyond a few feet from the cave. She growled back, which made his lips twitch, but the rest of his face held on to the scowl.

Like a good submissive, she sat in the middle of a patch of wildflowers and watched the sun fade into night.

"Addyson, you should go inside now," Hayden said softly as he came to a stop next to her.

She didn't want to, not until Keegan came back safe. She didn't know why, but she'd had a bad feeling since he left earlier that evening. Her nerves were like tiny live wires under her skin, sending pulses of unease and fear to every part of her body.

"In a little while," she said without looking away

from the tree line.

"Ten minutes," Hayden barked and walked off.

She felt her lips form a small smile. She liked Hayden. Underneath that hard-ass, iced shell of his, there was a heart warm and loyal. She'd seen him with the youth of den. It was true that all Pack members looked after and protected the younger and more vulnerable members, but she'd seen Hayden give a little more, spend more time, and comfort in a way she hadn't expected from the large, dangerous wolf Marshal.

A familiar scent drifted on the wind moments before Keegan emerged from the forest. She stood and waited. His gaze locked with hers, and damn if her body didn't heat up as her stomach did flips. He stalked toward her and stopped mere inches from her.

She cupped his face with both her hands then frowned. "You're bleeding."

Keegan pulled out of her grasp and said, "It's nothing."

"No, it's not nothing. Come on, let me look at it."

****

He let out a soft growl but followed her inside. The truth was that her stern words and the fire and spirit she'd shown pleased him. Hell, it was a damn turn-on, just like the sight of her slightly curvy hips as they swayed with each step she took into the living room.

She turned to face him when they reached the sofa and narrowed her eyes at him, as if knowing where his thoughts had gone. How was it that this woman could soothe the pain within him? She knew how to get inside him and ease the hurt he'd buried from losing his mate.

"Sit," she commanded as Will entered the room. He had his nose buried in the tablet in his hands.

Keegan peered over at the boy, making him look up. They locked gazes for a brief moment before the teen smirked and sat in the over-sized armchair across from them.

Shaking his head, Keegan sat on the sofa and watched Addyson as she left the room, only to return a moment later with the first aid kit. He was about to point out that he was an alpha leopard shifter and didn't run the risk of infection like humans did, but he refrained. There was no need to inflame her little temper by pointing out something she already knew. The temper she only showed around him, he mused.

Plus he liked the idea of her caring for him.

Her eyebrows drew together as she dabbed a cotton ball with a salve from an amber-colored jar. "What are you thinking?" she asked while focusing on her task.

He barely contained his flinch when she touched the cool cream to his wound. "How beautiful you are."

Will snickered from behind his tablet, but Keegan ignored him and continued to watch the way Addyson's cheeks colored. Although she tried to hide the way his words affected her, he saw it.

"Stop trying to get out of trouble." She fell silent, and her scent changed, indicating she was worried. He didn't push. She'd ask her questions when she was ready.

She placed a small bandage over the cut on his forehead then closed up the first aid kit. Without meeting his gaze, she said, "You fought with a mutant."

His heart stilled for a spit second, and he placed a finger under her chin, lifting it so her violet eyes stared into his. "I did."

It was his turn to look away, but he didn't remove

his hand from her chin. He needed the connection. Addyson had always grounded him on a level he'd never known. "I have a daughter."

Will stood and stretched while yawning loudly. The teen came over and kissed Addyson on the cheek. "Good night." When he straightened, he gave a short nod to Keegan and went to his room.

Keegan studied Addyson as she watched the kid walk off. "You've become attached to him," he said.

She peered at him, a flash of panic crossing her face before her expression became blank. "He's a good kid."

"I know. I've known since I first met him." She cocked her head in question, and he spoke before she could ask. "He needs to be challenged and questioned. It'd make him the strong Scribe I know he'll be some day."

She nodded and scanned his face. Silence surrounded them again, making him twitch with the need to do something, anything.

"I have a daughter," he said again.

She blinked. "Yes, I know Shay."

He shook his head. "No. I have another daughter. Felix stole her from me and Cate."

Addyson dropped shoulders and her eyes filled with unshed tears. "That's a terrible thing to do."

Keegan nodded and took her hand in his. "I believed all this time she was dead. The baby Cate birthed died right after birth. We buried our daughter... at least we thought we had."

Cool fingers touched his cheek, making him look into Addyson's face. "Felix is a bastard to the core." As soon as the words left her mouth, her eye widened. "Oh, God. No wonder Cate's image looked so familiar."

Keegan tightened his fingers around hers. "You've met Ana?"

Addyson shook her head. "Felix made sure I never made any kind of contact with her, but I saw her in passing during my captivity."

Anger bubbled up inside him. He knew from Kieran that Ana had been raised as one of two of the Onyx's princesses. That information gave Keegan hope that Ana had a somewhat happy life, if that was at all possible living inside a Pack that's main mission was to destroy others' lives.

"I met her."

Addyson let out a small gasp. "Did she...?"

He shook his head. "She doesn't know who I am."

He went on to tell her about the mutant and Ana killing it and his vow that he owed her a debt. By the time he finished speaking, they were both relaxed on the couch with Addyson snuggled into his side, her head resting on his chest.

Her scent tempted him like nothing else, made him crave things he hadn't in a very long time. He couldn't fight it any longer. The more time he spent with her, the more he wanted, no, needed.

His leopard refused to back down and became edgier with each denial. Both the man and cat were growing inpatient. Addyson Lewis belonged to him, and he was going to have her.

Soon.

CHAPTER NINE

Addyson sat at the kitchen table and watched the steam rise from her coffee. She couldn't sleep. The prior day's events kept replaying in her mind. Her heart ached for Keegan. He still held on to the pain of his loss, or was it the so-called betrayal?

Something just didn't settle right with her. Keegan's mate couldn't have turned her back on him and the Pack. Addyson refused to believe it to be the case.

The sound of shuffling feet drew her out of her thoughts. She turned her head as Will sat down next to her. "Morning. Did I wake you?"

He shook his head. "No, ma'am."

"Are you hungry? I made muffins."

His eyes brightened, and the corners of his mouth lifted. "Blueberry?"

Addyson laughed softly and ruffled his hair as she stood to go get the tray of muffins and pour him a glass of milk.

"Where are you from?"

She stilled briefly, surprised by the question. "What do you mean?"

"Where did you grow up?"

Addyson closed the milk carton and put it back in the fridge. "I don't remember my childhood."

Will drew his eyebrows together. "Not at all?"

Addyson shook her head. "Nope. Nevan, the Pack Empath and psychiatrist, said that my mind may have locked up my personal memories to preserve my own sense of reality."

A tic formed in his temple, and he took a breath before asking, "How long were you there?"

She shrugged. "About a hundred years." He fell silent, making Addyson peer over at him after taking her seat next to him. He picked at his muffin, and she could tell he was deep in thought. Covering his forearm with her hand, she said, "Now do you understand why my mind is broken?"

His gaze snapped up to hers. "You are not broken. You're just scared and need time to heal."

She meant to argue but stopped as she caught Keegan's oak-and-spice scent wrapping around her. A moment later she felt his hands press gently on her shoulders. Leaning down so his lips were inches from her ear, he whispered, "You're a very strong female, Addy."

Her heart fluttered rapidly behind her ribs, and for a second, she almost forgot how to breathe.

Keegan's weight lifted from her, and when he moved to walk around the table, she let out a breath she didn't remember holding. Sitting down across from her, he took a muffin from the plate and met her gaze with brown eyes so dark they looked black.

"Why don't you have Jared see if he can help you remember?" Keegan said casually.

Jared was the Pack Justice and possessed the ability to read people's memories through touch. Although it was possible that Jared could unlock her memories, there was the little issue she had with skin-to-skin contact.

Addyson shook her head. "I don't know if I want to remember."

Keegan narrowed his eyes at her. The stare was so intense she had to look away, her cat too much of a submissive to hold the connection.

She linked her fingers together on the table and focused on them as she told the two of them what she did know about her den. "Once, a few years before I escaped the Onyx den, I found a small clay bowl. It looked familiar, but somehow I knew it didn't belong to anyone in Onyx. So I touched it briefly with the tip of my index finger. I saw a younger version of myself holding the bowl while I sat propped against a large snow leopard. My father."

Tears burned her eyes as her vision grew blurry. She'd held onto that small happy memory, cherished it. It was the only piece of her past she had and the only hint of who her parents were before Onyx slaughtered them all.

Keegan placed his warm hand over hers, forcing her to lift her gaze to his. This time she held it. He didn't speak, just rubbed circles over her wrist with his thumb. It soothed her on a level that should have scared the life out of her.

Will set his empty glass on the table hard enough to snap Addyson out of whatever had just happened between her and Keegan. She peered over at the teen as he asked Keegan, "Can I go for a run? It's been awhile since I shifted."

Her leopard whimpered inside her head. She dropped her shoulders and glanced back at Keegan. He let out a sigh, stood, and held out his hand to her. "Come on. Let's go let our beasts out to play."

****

The relief mixed with excitement that passed over Addyson's face made Keegan want to pull her into his arms and claim every inch of her. It also pissed him the hell off that she hadn't been taking care of her leopard's needs.

When she placed her hand in his, he tugged her close so their bodies touched. "Why haven't you been taking care of this?"

It came out as a growl, and he sensed her cat wanting to submit to his. Damn it. With his free hand, he traced a finger down her cheek to her chin, where he lifted it gently to peer into her eyes.

Eyes that wouldn't meet his.

He pressed his forehead against hers and whispered, "Addy."

She relaxed slightly against him. "I'd shift at home, but only while within the den's protective wards. I was taken while on a hunt, caught in a net. So, I don't like to go out alone."

He hugged her closer, wrapping both arms around her. She was so strong; he knew that. He felt it when he was near her, but fear rode on her every action. She was too cautious. "You are free. Onyx will never have you again. I'll make sure of it."

Addyson pressed her hands against his chest and pushed. He let her go and allowed her to step back. Her brows dipped, and creases formed on her forehead. "I'm stronger than this, damn it."

It came out as a low mutter, but he heard it. He leaned in and nipped at her nose, bringing a shy smile to her sensual lips. He grabbed her hand and tugged her to the door. "You'll feel better after a good run."

Outside, the rays of the morning sun filtered through the trees, making the dew droplets sparkle. Beside him, Addyson took a deep breath, as if taking in the fragrances of the forest around them. Keegan too drew in the pine, oak, and other earthy scents, although he also wanted to make sure there weren't any rogues snooping about. As if on cue, Alec walked out of the trees and peered at the three of them before focusing on Keegan. "Anything wrong?" his son asked when he came to a stop beside him.

"No, just going for a run."

Alec gave a short nod and walked over to sit in one of the chairs under a shade tree a few yards from the entrance of the cave. Keegan shook his head as his son popped a pair of headphones in his ears. Alec had a way of appearing harmless right up until he struck.

A flash of movement to his left drew his attention to the gold and black leopard. Will stretched in his animal form then ran a circle around Keegan and Addyson.

Addyson laughed. "I think he is enjoying himself."

"It seems so." He placed a hand on her lower back. "Ready?"

She nodded while she took in a long, deep breath. Then she stripped down to her bra and panties. As shifters they didn't hold the same insecurities about nudity as humans. It was a fact of life, a natural state of being.

However, the sight of Addyson standing in front of him so incredibly beautiful and bare for the sentries Keegan smelled nearby to see made him want to cover her. His leopard didn't like her so exposed to them.

She peered at him from over her shoulder and smirked before she darted off into the forest, shifting into a snow leopard just before she disappeared behind the trees.

Keegan heard Alec chuckle as he stood and called out to Will. "Hey, Will. Come run with me. You don't want to be around the lovebirds."

Will let a playful growl then charged at Alec.

Keegan sent his son a telepathic "thanks" and shifted into his leopard, giving chase. His heart thumped against his ribcage, and he zipped around the trees. The wind blew through his fur, and he couldn't remember the last time he'd felt this great, this alive.

It was Addyson's doing. She had awakened something inside of him that went far beyond the urge to make her his.

He skidded to a halt when he saw her lying by a small stream. She was beautiful with her white coat dusted with black spots. He inched closer, careful not to startle her.

Her right ear twitched, but she didn't look his way, although he did notice how her body tensed with each step he took. He knew that if he moved to fast, she'd bolt. It was her nature no matter what hell she'd lived through at the hands of Onyx.

He came to a stop inches from her back. She stayed utterly still except for her tail, which twitched from side to side, but not out of annoyance. No, there was anxiety laced in her scent.

Moving around her, he lay down beside her and

nuzzled her neck and drew in her strawberry scent. Relief flooded him when she leaned into him, accepting him.

Taking a chance that he might regret, he shifted back to human form and whispered, "Shift for me."

She shuddered then, with a flash of soft white light, she shifted. He peered down at her, meeting her violet gaze. She was beautiful. She had high cheekbones, and a slightly rounded face that made her look much younger than the average shifter, most of which appeared to be in their early to mid thirties.

Addyson looked to be in her late twenties, although her eyes held secrets and a darkness that no one should ever know.

Addyson reached up and touched her fingertips to his lips. It was a bold move for her, a move that he didn't want to discourage. In fact he wanted her to know she didn't need his permission to touch him, pet him, anytime she wanted.

She studied him for several moments before asking, "Where's Will?"

"Alec is keeping him entertained." He inched his face closer to hers until their lips brushed together. Her breath caught, but she didn't pull away.

That was all the invitation he needed. He claimed her lips and was surprised she was ready for him, as if waiting for him to take charge. She opened her mouth, and he thrust his tongue inside, finding hers to dance with.

She threaded her fingers through his hair then fisted a handful to draw him closer.

Fuck.

She held a fire inside her that ignited the desire deep within him, the desire he'd thought had died until Addyson came into his life. He wanted her like he wanted no other.

He broke the kiss and rose over her. The violet in her eyes was so dark it made them almost black as she watched him cautiously. He kissed her nose then her chin and then her breastbone. She sucked in a breath, and he stilled.

"Addy?"

She ran her fingers through his hair, letting her nails lightly scrap over his scrap. "I'm fine. It's just...I've never..."

He pressed a kiss to her breast and said, "I'll be gentle." He moved his lips to her nipple and swiped his tongue over the tight bud.

"Keegan," she said on a gasp.

He trailed his fingers down her belly to her sex and stopped to let her catch her breath. "Are you okay?" She nodded, but he wasn't so sure. He could feel her anxiety and a hint of fear.

Slowly he dipped his fingers through her folds and groaned. "You're so wet."

She dug her nails into his bicep while he rubbed her clit in slow, circular movements.

"Too much?" he asked, not wanting to overload her senses.

"Yes, no. God, it feels good and a bit overwhelming."

"Do you want me to stop?"

She held his gaze and said, "No, not yet."

He bent down to capture her nipple between his teeth, causing her let out a cry of pleasure. He eased a finger inside her. She tensed for a moment then relaxed and started moving against him as he moved his finger in and out of her pussy.

God, she was so beautiful.

And all his.

His leopard growled in approval and nudged him to

take her, claim her as their mate.

No, he couldn't do that, not yet. Addyson would have to be eased into a mating. She also needed to fully understand what it meant to be mated to an alpha male as dominant as he was.

He slid a second finger inside her as he teased her nipple with his tongue. Her breathing came out in a gasp right before she cried out in release.

He lay down beside her and drew her into his arms and held her as the last shudder left her body. She laughed and said, "That was..."

He kissed her temple. "That was just a tease."

She laughed again and then fell silent. He wanted to demand that she tell him what was going on inside that head of hers, but he reined in the urge.

Finally she spoke. "You didn't...you weren't satisfied."

He squeezed her closer to him. "I'm fine. Pleasuring you is enough for now."

"But—"

He cut her off by biting down on her earlobe, which drew a squeak out of her. "No buts, Addy. Clear?"

She let out a breath, and he could hear the smile she tried to hide. "Yes, my Alpha."

He pinched her hip and growled, "Don't you forget it."

CHAPTER TEN

Ana jerked to the right and caught her sister, Sable, in the stomach with a shoulder and flipped her on her back. Sable landed with a grunt then started laughing.

"Well done, little sis."

Ana straightened and smirked at her sister. "I got you that time."

Sable held up her hand. Ana grabbed it and jerked her to a stand. "I was tired."

Ana laughed. "Excuses, excuses."

Ana walked over to the one of the benches positioned around the edges of the large gym, which was located in the middle of the Onyx den. After she sat, she grabbed her water bottle and took a drink as she watched Sable do the same.

Sable wasn't her real sister. She was Ana's adopted

sister. Ana had known this all her life, although she never mentioned it out of fear of what her father would say. That was until today. She couldn't get the man she'd helped in the woods out of her mind. Of course she knew he was the Alpha of Ashwood and supposedly her enemy, according to the stories her father had told her growing up.

Yet, the man—Keegan—was not a threat to her. She couldn't understand how she knew that, but she did. Deep inside her soul, she sensed he would never harm her. No matter who she was and where she came from.

Sable sat beside her and leaned her shoulder against Ana's. "What's on your mind?"

Ana peered over at Sable and narrowed her eyes. "Am I really that easy to read?"

Sable shrugged. "No, but I know when something is bothering you."

Ana smiled and looked around the empty gym. "Could we talk somewhere more private?" she asked in a low whisper, meant only for Sable to hear.

Sable stood, stretched her lean body, and said, "Come back to my place, and I'll fix us dinner."

Ana rose and followed her sister out of the gym and across the center of the den to the private section of living quarters for the senior officers. Sable's apartment was at the end of the corridor that branched off from the others. Sable had told Ana that the space was designed for the Alpha of the Pack, but Felix refused to stay there. Why Ana didn't know, but she'd guess it was because their father believed he was above anyone else.

No, the Alpha of Onyx stayed in a large cabin just outside the den. It was just one the many things that bugged Ana about her adopted father.

When they reached Sable's door, Ana caught an all-too-familiar scent in the damp air of the cavern tunnel.

Rich, spicy, and belonging to the one male who could break her heart.

Kieran Michaels rounded the corner, and he didn't look pleased. His dark brows dipped to cause a crease in his forehead, and there was a tic in his jaw that indicated he was clenching his teeth. He looked deadly and hot as hell.

Kieran stopped a few feet from them and held Ana's gaze as he spoke to Sable. "Two mutants were found dead an hour ago."

Ana stilled, and her heart sank into her stomach. This would make the third time she had been caught outside the den. Each time before, Sable had stepped up and saved her from a beating from their father. Sable had always taken the punishment for Ana's fuckups.

Sable growled low and said, "Kieran, why don't you join us for an early dinner?"

Kieran snapped his gaze toward Sable and studied her for a long moment before he turned to go inside Sable's apartment.

Once inside, Ana felt the tension fill the room. Kieran stood against the far wall with his arms crossed. Ana took a seat on the sofa and took a deep breath. "I killed the mutants," she said softly.

Sable dropped into the chair across from her. "We know that. The problem is you can't continue to do it. I don't like the dumbass animals any more than you do."

Kieran cleared his throat, forcing her to look at him. Damn. He knew she wasn't alone in the forest. He most likely smelled Keegan on her. Kieran, after all, was a possessive male and had no issues with letting everyone know Ana was his.

"They creep me out and follow me. Besides, I don't like the way they look at me." She sat back on the sofa, refusing to meet Kieran's stare. He wasn't going to like what she told him next. "The first one I killed...touched me."

Kieran's growl rumbled through the room, making her peer up at him. His hands were fisted by his side and his mouth set in a hard line. "How did he touch you?"

"Does it matter? I killed him. None of them has messed with me since."

Sable asked, "And what about the second one?"

Ana shrugged. "He saw me use my ability. I have to get out of the den and expend the energy buildup. I was afraid he'd tell father. Sable, you were the one who told me father can't know about my gift to control the natural elements."

Sable crossed her arms over her chest. "You are also not to be alone. It's for you're own safety."

Kieran nodded in agreement with Sable. "What about today?"

She met his stare and said, "I saved a man's life today." He gave her a raised brow for her to continue. She took a deep breath, then let it out slowly. "I met the Elder of Ashwood."

Sable jumped up from her seat and started pacing. "What did he say? Shit, this is bad."

Kieran grabbed Sable's upper arm as she passed by him, halting her. "We'll deal with it." He peered at Ana again. "Tell us what happened."

Ana pursed her lips. Anger started to build inside her. They were hiding something from her. The two people she'd thought she could trust in this dysfunctional Pack had withheld information from her. It not only pissed her the hell off, but it hurt.

"I saved his life from the mutant, and now he owes me a favor." She wasn't going to tell them about his strange reaction to her. Keegan had seemed to recognize her, but that was impossible. She'd spent her whole life locked up inside the Onyx den.

Well, not actually locked up, but close enough in her opinion. She was forbidden to leave the secure walls of the mountain where the den was located.

Kieran growled. "Is that all he said? He owes you a favor?"

"Yes."

Sable sat beside her and took her hand. Ana's pulse picked up, and dread filled her belly. Sable had kicked into mother mode. This couldn't be good.

"There isn't any easy way to say this but to just spit it out. Since you know you're adopted, and you know of Felix's twisted way of ruling the Pack..." Kieran let out a warning growl, but Sable didn't flinch. She didn't even acknowledge him. "Anyway, Keegan Andrews is your real father."

Ana jerked her hands away from Sable and stood. Kieran moved closer to her, and she snapped her gaze to him, fury building inside her. "You knew this? Both of you. I knew there was something you weren't telling me. Damn it. My whole life. I could have had a different life."

Her head started to hurt. Images of Keegan in the forest fighting the mutant flashed in her mind. She'd felt a connection to him but didn't know what it was. He wasn't Pack. Yet, now they were saying he was her father.

She started to shake, and then Kieran's warm, strong arms wrapped around her from behind. He pressed a kiss to her temple and whispered, "I'm a spy for the Ashwood Falls Packs."

She sagged against him. "Why am I not surprised? What else are you two keeping from me?"

Sable sighed and sat back against the couch.

"Nothing. You already know about the rebels and my involvement."

Ana snorted. Sable wasn't only involved; she was their freaking leader.

"Tell me everything. I have a right to know."

Sable nodded. "You'll only want to kill Father more than you already do."

Ana smiled. "I don't think that's possible."

****

Keegan lay across the king-sized bed and watched Addyson step out of the bathroom. Water droplets rolled down her cheek to her neck and disappeared into the towel she'd wrapped around herself. He fought the urge to snatch the towel from her so he could watch the water continue its journey down her beautiful, slightly curvy body.

She lifted her violet gaze to him, and one side of her mouth lifted in a smirk. "What?"

He patted the bed. "Come here."

"Oh, no. We are going to talk about Cate and Ana."

He growled and rolled to lie on his back. He had agreed to let her help him decipher the vision she'd had to see if there were any truths in the theory that Cate had been controlled. "Where is that submissive cat?"

Addyson climbed on the bed and lay next to him. "She's decided she likes playing with you."

He turned his head to peer at her profile and realized she'd smiled more today than he'd ever seen her do. He'd have to make sure she continued to smile, always. "You're beautiful when you smile, and when you're mad."

"Well, you mister, make me both happy and furious all at the same time."

He chuckled and pulled her to lie across his chest. "I plan to do both for a very long time."

Silence filled the room, and he waited for the ache in his chest to overpower his ability to think rationally. It never came. Instead, his leopard purred and rubbed against his chest where Addyson snuggled.

Of course the cat would. He'd already claimed her as his mate. The man was just now starting to accept it.

He kissed the top of her head. "So, Felix can control minds."

"Yes. He did it to me until I finally let my mind break, and then he said I gave him headaches."

Keegan didn't bother to hold back his growl. "Felix will die one day. It'll be one day soon if I get my hands on him."

She smoothed her palm over his chest and threaded her fingers through the light dust of chest hair. "He rules through mind control and fear."

Keegan already knew this. Well, the fear part. The mind control was new knowledge. He wondered if Kieran knew. Did it even matter?

"Did you know Felix had an adopted daughter?"

Addyson shrugged. "I heard rumors. They mentioned some female by the name of Zorana and how she was off limits to everyone. It really didn't make any senses to me at the time."

Zorana. It was the name Cate had picked out. She said it sounded exotic and beautiful. Felix must have pulled the name out of her mind. Keegan grounded his molars and tried to calm himself. "Addy, you know I'll have to go for a run after this conversation. I'm not used to facing all these emotions and not kill something."

She released a small sigh. "I know. Thanks for trying.

I do believe it will help."

"Have you been hanging out with Nevan?"

She laughed. "I've been speaking with him. He comes by the house. We have tea and talk."

Keegan hugged her close. "That's good. Is it helping?"

"Yes, I think it's why I can now try to create my shields with Will's help."

He smiled. The human psychiatrist now mated to the leopard Healer had proven himself and had helped many Pack members deal with issues in the short time he'd been in the den. Keegan was glad to have him.

His phone rang, drawing him out of his thoughts. He picked it up after the second ring. "This better be good," he snapped.

"She wants to meet with you," Kieran said, not at all fazed by Keegan's tone.

Keegan stopped breathing for a second. "What? You told her?"

Kieran laughed. "She's as smart and stubborn as you are."

Keegan was too stunned to reply with a smartass comment. "Okay. What time?"

"Mid-morning, our usual meeting place."

Keegan hung up the phone and met Addyson's smiling face. "This is good, right?"

He kissed her forehead. "I hope so."

God, he hoped so. The last thing he needed was to walk into a trap.

CHAPTER ELEVEN

Keegan arrived at a small underground waterfall about a mile north of Ashwood territory. It was the small section of neutral land between his and what used to be Hunter Ridge Pack territory, just over the Tennessee boarder. Keegan loved to come here as boy and not many knew about the waterfall tucked inside a cavern in the earth.

He sat on a large bolder and listened to the water roar as it fell rapidly over rock and into the stream below it. Until he'd met Addyson, this place had been his only solitude, the only time he could drop his shields and not hear others' thoughts.

He scented Kieran before the male dropped down inside the cave. Keegan gave the male a short nod in greeting. Kieran returned the gesture then a scowl crossed his face as Ana dropped in behind him.

"Ana."

She smiled, patted Kieran on the shoulder, and walked around him. "You said this place was safe." She peered around in awe. "This is cool and beautiful."

The ache, now dull to the point that it didn't put his cat on edge, surfaced at the sight of her. "You look just like her."

Ana stopped and looked right at him. She drew her eyebrows together. "It pains you."

It wasn't a question, but he answered anyway. "It does, but seeing you gives me hope."

She narrowed her eyes at him and moved to sit on the rock across from him. Kieran shifted closer, but she ignored him. "How so?"

Keegan lifted his gaze to Kieran. "How much did you tell her?"

"That Felix stole her from you and Cate at birth. Nothing else. I felt it was your job to tell her." Kieran's gaze lowered to Ana. "I hope she understands why I couldn't tell her."

Ana sighed. "Kieran and Sable have withheld information from me my whole life. I don't like to be lied to."

Keegan smiled, despite sensing the growing bond between Kieran and Ana. "There is a difference between lying to deceive and lying to protect."

She pursued her lips. "It's still lying, and I don't like it."

Keegan held in his laugh. It was so amazing how much she was like Cate, yet held many of his own traits. "Your mother betrayed the Pack by feeding information to Felix then took her own life to spare me from doing it."

Ana fell silent and stared into the water. "That's so

sad."

Keegan nodded. "Yeah, but the Pack believes she was killed by the rogues."

She drew back and studied him. He wasn't sure if it was because of the rogue comment or the fact that he'd admitted to lying to his Pack. "Not all of us are rogues." She stood and walked over to stand beneath the cave entrance and stopped. Turning around to face him, she added in a softer tone, "Lying to your Pack about their Alpha female wasn't wrong. I'm guessing they loved her as much as you did."

She stepped forward to stand beside Kieran. "I've always known that I didn't belong in Onyx. I hate Felix. He might have raised me, but he was never a father to me or Sable. We were his soldiers to be used to bring down his own race."

She fisted her hands beside her, and the water froze in mid-fall. Keegan jumped up and looked at the water then at Ana. He laughed and said, "Your mother had a quarter earth witch in her. She could control the elements if she focused hard enough. The ability must have passed on to you."

Ana dropped her shoulders, and the water started moving again. "I didn't start having the ability until after my first shift at thirteen. Sable helped me hide it from Felix. Sometimes I have to go outside to expend extra energy. And I always have to watch my temper and emotions while around others in the den."

Keegan cut a gaze to Kieran. "She needs to get out of the den. Take her to Ashwood. I'll call Blaine so he'll be expecting you."

Kieran shook his head. "Not tonight. We were seen leaving the den together, which I can explain as a training exercise. So Felix will be expecting her to return to the den."

Fuck. "You have three days to come up with some kind of plan to get her out of that hell of a den," Keegan growled.

Kieran growled back and took a step forward. "You aren't my Alpha anymore. Blaine is."

Keegan felt his lips twitch. "Should I call him to tell him his baby sister is alive and in Onyx?"

Ana crossed her arms over her chest. "Hello. I'm still here and able to make my own decisions. Who the hell is Blaine?"

Kieran answered her question before Keegan could. "He's one of your brothers and the new leopard Alpha of Ashwood Falls."

Ana dipped her brows and looked from Kieran the Keegan. "One of my brothers? How many do I have?"

Keegan moved past her to stand under the opening of the cavern. "You have two brothers, Blaine and Alec, and an adopted sister, Shay."

"There is so much I must know, but Kieran is right. I should be getting back soon." She walked over to Keegan and touched his cheek with her fingers. "We'll be at Ashwood tomorrow evening. I'll make sure of it."

Before she turned away, Keegan took out his phone and snapped a picture of her.

"What was that for?"

Keegan smiled. "I need proof for Blaine. Let's just say he'll need it."

Ana rolled her eyes, but didn't hide the smile that formed as she hopped up on the ledge under the opening and climbed out of underground cave. Kieran moved in behind her, only to stop and peer back at Keegan. "She's strong. She's has her mother's fire and love for life, and her father's stubbornness."

Keegan smiled as Kieran turned and climbed out of the hole. Ana, the daughter he'd lost, was coming home.

The hole in his soul started to knit together, healing the pain he'd carried for far too long.

As for Felix, well, the leopard would get what was coming to him.

Once above ground, Keegan telepathically connected with Blaine. "Meet me at the safe house in ten and bring Cam. We're going rogue hunting."

****

Felix paced his large living room, hands fisted at his side and blood boiling in his veins. How dare she lie to him? His own daughter.

"Are you sure she's heading the operation?" he gritted out to his Marshal, Vance.

"I am. I have spies all over the den. Besides, I heard one of her officers mention it."

Felix snapped his gaze to Vance. "That's not right. Sable is much too smart and lethal to allow her followers to speak of it inside the den."

Vance crossed his arms as he leaned against the wall. "Even if it was Ana who spoke?"

Felix growled, the sound echoing off the walls. "Let me guess. She was talking to the Ashwood spy."

Vance nodded, and it only infuriated him more. Yes, he'd known Kieran was a spy for Keegan and Luna for several months. Felix had noticed a crack in the mental wall the male kept over his mind and used it to slip in. He was able to get enough information to tell him Kieran wasn't only a spy, but Ana's mate.

Shit kept getting better and better.

It appeared he'd have to take control of the situation and show both Kieran and Ashwood not to fuck with the Onyx Alpha.

Meeting his Marshal's gaze, Felix said, "It's time to eliminate the problem. Zorana is no longer useful to me."

Vance straightened. "What about Sable?"

Felix closed his eyes. There was a time he'd have protected his daughter at all cost, but this was a war and sacrifices had to be made. Besides, he had no doubt that, given the chance, his daughter would kill him.

"Sable has chosen her side."

CHAPTER TWELVE

Addyson had just stepped out of the shower when she heard Blaine's voice from the living room. Odd, she wasn't aware he'd be stopping by, and she wasn't sure how long Keegan would be gone.

She dressed and towel-dried her hair before making her way to the living room. Addyson made eye contact with Cameron for a brief moment. The female enforcer sat on the sofa next to Blaine and talked quietly with Will. Cam had her long black hair pulled back in a ponytail, and she wore a pair of faded blue jeans and a soft blue T-shirt.

Shifting her gaze, she caught Blaine's gray stare, which made her instantly look away. Her submissive cat was still not comfortable meeting the new Alpha's gaze. Direct eye contact with a dominant could be taken as a challenge.

Addyson instead focused on Will, who sat on the arm of the sofa next to Cam. "No offense, but why are you here? Has something happen?" Oh, God, if the den was attacked...

No, that wasn't right. Her imagination was running amuck. The Alpha pair, well, two of a triad, could just be there for a visit with Keegan.

Blaine chuckled and sat back in the sofa. "My father told us to meet him here. I take it you don't know why, do you?"

Shit. What was she supposed to say? She wasn't even sure if Blaine knew about his long lost, believed-dead, sister. "I have a guess on what it's about, but I think you should hear it from your father."

Blaine nodded. "Fair enough."

Addyson relaxed a little. "Would you like something to drink?"

Before anyone could answer, the door to the cave slid opened, and damn if her heart didn't flip at the sight of Keegan. Then concern filled her mind. His brows were drawn together causing his forehead to crinkle. A tic in his temples told her he was clenching his jaw. However, when his gaze met hers, she saw his pain. She wanted to go to him, wrap her arms around him, and soothe away any of the aliments that darkened his mood.

As if knowing what she was thinking, he walked straight to her, pulled her to a stand, and sat in the chair, pulling her into his lap. She stiffened and he made soothing circular motions on her back, making her relax and lean into his touch.

When she peered over at Blaine, Addyson noticed the male wasn't surprised by Keegan's affection. That made her wonder just how long Blaine had known about her being his father's mate. It couldn't have been too long.

Hell, it was all still so new to Addyson.

Keegan spoke after a long moment, and Addyson wasn't sure if the silence was to find the right words to tell his son of a sister he'd never known or something else. "I just came back from meeting with Kieran. We may have to pull a rescue."

Blaine raised a brow. "To rescue Kieran? Has he gone soft over the years in Onyx?"

Keegan's lips twitched then dipped into a frown. "Not for Kieran. For your sister."

Blaine froze and stared at his father with a narrowed-eyed glare. "My sister is safe with her very overprotective mate."

Keegan replied, with a tone void of emotion. "Zorana."

Blaine's features hardened, and he growled, "I'm not in the mood for jokes or playing games with you. Zorana died at birth."

The tension surging through the room made Addyson's leopard whimper and curl into a ball. Addyson didn't blame her; she wanted to curl up somewhere safe as well. Keegan must have sensed the shift in her mood, for he pulled her closer to him and massaged her scalp, calming her and the cat within.

"Believe me, son, I would never joke about this. You need to calm down and think. Am I really that cruel?" Keegan said through his teeth then took out his phone and tossed it to Blaine. "Pull up the first image. I took that before returning here because somehow I knew you'd need proof."

Blaine opened the file and stared for several moments before responding. "Fuck me. This isn't possible. She has to be, what? Thirty-eight?"

Keegan nodded. "She's been raised in the Onyx den as Felix's daughter. She knew she was adopted and was told her parents died when she was born."

Blaine handed the phone back to Keegan. "So when are we getting her out of there?"

"Tomorrow evening. If she doesn't call me by seven, then we go in."

Blaine narrowed his eyes and pursed his lips. "And you know where the Onyx den is?"

Keegan nodded and Blaine studied his father for several long moments before finally speaking. "I don't like it. I can't order the enforcers to go into a rogue den full of half crazed mutants."

"Then I'll go by myself."

A tic formed in Blaine's temple. "I can't allow you to do that. There are laws we must follow. Laws you of all people know like your own eye color."

Keegan nudged Addyson to get up. She did and moved to stand next to the chair, allowing Keegan room to stand. He looked at his son and said, "We do this my way. After my mate and my daughter are safe, then I'll start taking orders from you."

****

It was an hour before sunset when Alec returned from teaching the youth training class. As the new Marshal, he had to recruit the new soldiers and train them, as well as lead the enforcers.

Alec entered the cave and dropped down on the couch. "So Blaine said you have something to tell me."

Keegan lifted his head from the map he had sprawled out on the coffee table to meet Alec's gaze. Keegan wasn't surprised that Blaine hadn't filled his brother in on Ana. Blaine might be the hotheaded son, but it was

Alec who had the potential to be the ticking bomb, just like his father.

So, yeah, Blaine was right. Keegan had to be the one to tell Alec.

"Your sister didn't die at birth."

Alec released a low growl but otherwise sat perfectly still. "What?"

Keegan didn't answer. He let Alec absorb the news and studied the map again.

After what seemed like minutes, Alec asked, "Felix had her stolen?"

Keegan nodded. One thing about Alec was his ability to sense things and fill in the blanks. Keegan never had to explain things to him, not even as a child.

After another brief moment of silence, Alec growled out, "That fucking Onyx bastard will die."

Keegan folded the map and tucked it in the drawer of the coffee table. "Yep." He sat back and peered at Alec. Keegan could feel Alec's leopard, as well as the man, grow more on edge. Not that he blamed him. Keegan was still pissed about the whole issue with Ana. It made him wonder just how far Felix was planning on going. Better yet, what was the point of taking Ana in the first place?

"Why don't you take Will out for a run? The kid needs to get out of the cave for a bit."

Alec's expression softened a little then he called out, "William!"

When the kid appeared in the entranceway from the hall, Alec stood and said, "Come hunting with me."

Keegan watched as the two walk to the door, slid it open, stripped off their clothes, and shifted into their leopard forms.

"They sure have taken to each other."

Keegan turned to Addyson as she walked into the

living room and smiled. "Yes. Alec didn't take the news of Ana's death after birth well. He'd formed a bond with her before she was even born. Made all kinds of plans of making her tough and promised she'd be safe."

Addyson stepped into his embrace, resting her head on his shoulder, as if sensing he needed her touch. "Wouldn't he have sensed that she was still alive?"

"Felix must have done something to break the bond between Ana and Cate. It's the only thing that makes sense."

Addyson placed her palm over his heart. "Once the mother/daughter bond was broken, any other bond would break too." She let out a soft growl that both surprised Keegan and turned him on at the same time. "I really hate Felix. The male must die."

Keegan lifted her chin so he could peer into her violet eyes. "He will get what's coming to him, but I do believe you have to stand in line."

She smiled and stood on her toes and kissed his chin. "Make me forget all the ugliness."

He scooped her up in his arms and turned toward their bedroom. "Anything, mate of mine."

CHAPTER THIRTEEN

Addyson was still wondering where that bold female had come from as Keegan laid her down in the bed they shared but hadn't made love in. Until now.

Keegan peered down at her, his brown eyes darkening with desire. "Are you sure about this?"

Her stomach flipped, and her heart beat louder. At least it sounded that way to her. "Yes. I've denied myself this pleasure for far too long because I was afraid of what it would do to me. I don't want to be afraid anymore. I trust you to catch me if I fall."

He kissed her nose. "I'll always be here to catch you."

She didn't have time to reply before his mouth came down on hers in a searing kiss that sent pinpricks of desire rushing over her skin. His tongue slipped between her lips and she opened to allow it inside to tangle with hers. He tasted as divine as he smelled, making her want more of this male.

She ran her nails lightly up his back to his hair and pulled out the rubber band that held his long dark hair. The silky strains fell over his shoulder and brushed against hers.

He broke the kiss and kissed his way down her neck to her collarbone before rising. Lifting her into a sitting position, he removed her shirt and bra and tossed them to the floor. She gasped when he captured one nipple in his mouth and teased the sensitive nub. A wave of dizzying pleasure washed over her, stopping her ability to speak.

Her heart sped up when Keegan abandoned her breast and trailed light kisses down her stomach. Sensation rippled through every inch of her, making it hard to concentrate. Her skin felt as though it were on fire, except there was no pain, just heat and pleasure. God, there was so much pleasure she thought she'd burst.

Keegan raised his head from her abdomen. "Addy?"

"I'm here."

"We can stop..."

She shook her head. "No. Please."

Great, she was panting and begging.

Keegan growled low, but it sounded like a purr was mixed into the sound, sensual and demanding all at once. He rose up on his knees, and she watched as he unbuttoned her jeans and removed them along with her panties. When he let the garments fall to the floor and met her gaze, she gasped as his cat peered out of those brown eyes.

She reached up and ran her fingers through his hair as he lowered his mouth to press against her skin and trailed feather-like kisses down her stomach until his mouth covered her clit. She tensed for a brief second then moaned as his tongue teased the bundle of nerves.

Pleasure overpowered the fear and worry, making Keegan and what he was doing to her the only things she thought about.

She gasped and fisted her hand in his hair when he inserted a finger inside her. A rush of emotions mixed with intense pleasure burned through her. It was as if her own pleasure was doubled, then she felt it. A tiny connection to Keegan. His emotions, his desire, and his pleasure washed over her.

She'd never connected with anyone like this. It was almost too much sensation, too much Keegan. Her senses were all over the place, her mind tried to make sense of it. The full on skin contact sparked her psychic gift to life, but a vision didn't slam into her like with others. No, touching Keegan and being with him like this left her with only pleasure and sensations that left her mindless in a very good way. She didn't want it to end. Even if it meant she'd go insane with sensory overload.

Keegan slid another finger inside her, drawing a gasp from her. She bucked her hips and fisted the sheets and tried to crawl backward to break the contact, if for only a moment. Keegan grabbed her hips, holding her in place.

God, the man was going to kill her with the desire he ignited inside her. Heat covered her body, and she didn't know how much more of this slow, pleasurable torture she could take.

He pumped his fingers in and out faster and harder until she screamed his name as an orgasm tore through her.

Panting and unable to move, she watched as Keegan withdrew his fingers and crawled up her body, a grin on his face.

She rolled her eyes and tried not to smile. That was too hard, especially when she'd just had the best orgasm ever. "I can't move. I'm useless now, and it's all your fault."

He chuckled and swiped his tongue over a nipple, drawing another moan from her. "Useless, huh? I could have my way with you, and you can't do anything about it."

Good Lord, he didn't know just how true that was.

He continued his slow, graceful crawl up her torso until his face was level with hers. She cupped his face and pulled him down for a kiss. He growled, which did nothing but excite her even more.

She circled her ankles around the backs of his thighs and tugged him closer until his erection pressed into her through his jeans. She scowled. "Take the jeans off."

The corners of his mouth lifted in a sensual smile. "Is my submissive giving orders?"

"Yes," she said, trying to sound firm, but failed. She swore it had sounded firmer in her head.

He leaned down to place his lips on her ear and whispered, "Say please."

Her heart thumped faster, and heat pooled between her legs. She fought with her cat for a few moments, wanting to be a little defiant. Finally losing to her submissive nature, she purred out her reply. "Please."

His answer was a devilish smirk that sent a shiver through her. He got off the bed and removed his clothes then settled himself between her legs. Her heart kicked up again, and anticipation ran through her veins, warming her even more and intensifying her need to be possessed by this man.

He pressed his lips to hers in a brief, but soft, kiss as he cradled her head between his hands. "You're my mate, and the urge to bond with you is too strong."

It was a warning, and she knew he wouldn't be able to stop what was second nature to them. She lifted her head and kissed him briefly on the mouth then nipped at his chin. "I'm yours, Keegan. Always."

His features softened in what she swore was relief, but really what did this gorgeous alpha male have to worry about? Did he actually believe she'd turn him away now?

The male was crazy to think so.

She wrapped her arms around his neck and whispered, "You're mine as I am yours. I'll wait for you. No matter how long it takes. I'm here when you're ready to mate."

He struck so fast and hard she gasped. Pain and pleasure overtook her as his fangs scored her neck at the same time he thrust into her. There was no more rational thought. No worries that Keegan would never claim her, because he did.

In the best possible way.

A fiery sensation raced inside her as well as over her skin. Keegan's scent intensified, and she inhaled it, loving everything about it, about this male.

She moved against him as he thrust into her over and over, and she waited for panic to set in at the overload of sensations, but the pleasure built until she was consumed by it, unable to think about anything but the way Keegan was loving her.

And he did love her. She felt it now. The tiny threads that had connected them earlier strengthened, forming a bond that would bind them to each other for the rest of their existence.

The mating bond snapped into place at the same time they both cried out in release.

CHAPTER FOURTEEN

Addyson eased out of bed, careful not to wake Keegan as she dressed and made her way to the kitchen to make coffee. She leaned against the counter and waited as the coffee pot did its thing. Images of the night before swirled in her head, bringing a smile to her face that she couldn't get rid of if she wanted. And she didn't want to, ever.

Keegan had shown her pleasure she'd never known. In fact her skin still tingled from his touch and the way he held her as they slept.

When the coffee pot gurgled the last of the water through the grounds, she fixed a cup and walked outside. Birds chirped happily in the trees, making her smile widened. It was a beautiful morning with clear blue skies and a cool breeze blowing through the trees.

She heard a lazy growl above her. "Morning, Alec."

His answer was a flick of his tail against the branch he stretched out on. She started to walk into the forest, but stopped when Alec jumped down in front of her, bearing his teeth. Her cat backed away from the Beta and urged her to do the same. But the woman wanted a moment of independence.

"I'm going for a walk. I won't go too far." When he didn't move, she dropped her head. "Please? I need to roam by myself, even if it's just for a bit."

He growled again, but stepped aside. She knelt down and ran a hand over his large gold and black head. Times like these were the only time she was able to have contact with others. She didn't understand it fully, but guessed that the fur acted like a buffer in the same way her gloves did. Another theory was that while in animal form, they were at their purest of hearts, or it could be that her gift just didn't work on animals. Shifters in animal form included.

"I'll be careful. Promise. Give me twenty minutes, then you can come look for me. Deal?"

He raised his head and lowered it in a nod then butted his head against her chin. She gave him scratch under the chin and rose to take her walk. All the while she could feel Alec's gaze on her. She didn't care. She was going to do this and show herself and her cat that they can go for a short walk on their own, without fear.

It felt great.

A few yards in the heavy wooded area she caught movement from the corner of eye. Her heart stilled for a brief moment and her stomach sank to her knees. Fear laid hot and heavy in her chest. Shit. She should turn back.

Then a woman stepped out from behind a tree and Addyson recognized her instantly.

"Ana," she breathed.

Ana cocked her head and narrowed her eyes. "You look familiar."

"I'm Addyson. The scribe Felix held captive."

Ana frowned. "I hate what he's done. What about the boy? Will, I think that's his name."

"He's safe."

Ana sighed. "That's good." She sniffed the air, then smiled. "You smell like Keegan."

Addyson relaxed a little. "Come walk with me?"

"Okay."

They walked in silence for several minutes. It seemed like an hour, but Addyson knew that wasn't right. Alec hadn't come after her yet. Then again she didn't expect the male to wait the full twenty minutes either.

Addyson finally broke the silence. "Were you the one who let Will go?"

Ana laughed. "Yep. How did you know?"

"A guess. I'm good at reading emotions. Did you let Graham go to?"

"Who?"

"The puma Felix had a few months ago."

Ana shook her head. "That was Sable."

"Why? I mean, I don't understand. You both are his daughters. Well, at least Sable is."

The other female shrugged. "Felix is not well in the head. He's mad, if not completely insane. We don't like what he's done to the Pack and what he's still doing. We try to help those we can. The others, the ones who refuse us, are on their own."

Addyson thought about it for a few moments. It made sense, in a way. She was about to ask another question when Ana grabbed her hand and pulled her into a group of shrubs. Addyson cried out as visions of Ana being held by two mutants while another man whipped her repeatedly. Addyson felt every sting from the leather as it sliced into Ana's back.

"Addyson!"

She could hear someone calling her name, but couldn't see anyone through the pain.

"Listen to me. Focus on something. Keegan. Picture Keegan and you, in your mind, then wrap a bubble around the two of two."

Ana's voice finally cut through the haze, making the vision fade slightly. Doing as the female said, Addyson imagined standing in Keegan's arms and wrapped a clear bubble around them, blocking out everything.

Then vision disappeared, leaving behind a peace she'd hadn't experienced in a very long time. She met Ana's gaze, and asked, "How?"

"It's something Sable taught me to keep Felix out of my head. All I have to do is think of my mate, safe in his arms, and wrapped in a bubble, my mind is safe from mind control."

Addyson smiled wide. The bubble around her mind was holding and was a lot stronger than the one she created with Tanner and Blaine a day ago. Tentatively she touched Ana on the arm. Nothing happen. Excitement shot through her, but quickly faded when she recalled the vision she had.

"Do they...punish you often?"

Ana shot her a quick look of confusion, then dropped her head. "Not if Sable or Kieran is around. Father... Felix orders it when I "step out of line". It seems lately the smallest things set him off."

Before Addyson could say another word, Ana grabbed her hand again and pulled her further into woods. Addyson was about to ask what the deal was until the sickly sweet scent of mutants reached her nose.

Ana turned to her and whispered, "You need to get

out of here."

Addyson shook her head. She liked Ana. "Come with me."

"I can't. I'll be okay. Just go."

Ana gave her a little push toward the opposite direction where they heard the mutants. Addyson stumbled, then turned and ran.

She'd bring back help.

She skidded to a halt when a large mutant stepped into her path. The beast, like the others of his kind, was ugly, something straight out of a horror movie. It made her wonder if the writers of those werewolf movies had actually had a run in with one of Felix's mutants.

She darted to the left and dodged his arm, but was too slow when he gave chase. The half-man, half-wolf grabbed her from behind, threw her over his shoulder, and carried her back toward where she left Ana. Addyson screamed, praying that Alec ignored her plea for time alone and came looking for her.

****

Keegan woke with a start. He sat straight up in bed and looked around then found the reason he'd woken. Addyson wasn't there. Stretching out his senses, he tried to find her. If she was in the cave, he'd know it. Cold dread shot up his spine when the only person he sensed inside the cave was Will, sound asleep in his room.

He jumped out of bed and, not brothering with clothes, he rushed to the bedroom door. His phone rang as he reached the hall, causing him to turn around to get it. "Yeah," he barked into the cell phone.

"Ana is gone." Kieran's pissed-off voice, full of alarm, shot through the line.

"So is Addyson."

Fuck, this wasn't good. How the hell had she gotten out of the cave undetected?

All of a sudden, like someone flipped a switch, cold fear crawled up his spine. Then Alec broke into his thoughts. "Addyson's been taken by mutant. I'm on his tail. You need to get here, fast."

Fuck. Alec didn't need to tell him where "here" was. Keegan could find the location through the bond with his son, and now through the mating bond with Addyson.

"They're close to the waterfall."

Kieran grunted and said, "Why?"

"Don't know. Alec said a mutant has Addyson. I'm leaving now." Keegan hung up the phone without another word, dressed, and headed to the underground waterfall.

When he arrived a few feet from the hidden entrance to the waterfall, his heart dropped to his feet. Ana and Alec were engaged in a fight with two mutants. Although Ana was holding her own, Keegan could tell she was distracted. Scanning the area, he found Addyson crouched down behind a large rock.

Ana kept moving closer to the other female as she side kicked one mutant in the chest, knocking him backward a few steps.

"Don't let them bite you," Ana warned Alec.

"Yeah, no shit." Alec shot back and ducked a punch the half-wolf creature threw at him. A split second later the mutant swiped his feet from under him, sending him on his back.

Keegan charged the creature and hit him full force in the stomach. They fell to the ground, and Keegan straddled him and let his claws out. Keegan might not have the Alpha magick, but he still had the ability to hold onto a mid-shift longer than others. He swiped his claw out, scratching the mutant across the face.

He caught the sight of Kieran rushing by to barrel into another mutant who'd joined the party. Next to him, a shot fired, and then blood sprayed over his T-shirt. The mutant under him went limp. Keegan moved his gaze up to see Addyson holding a gun still aimed at the mutant.

Keegan stood, went to her, and took the gun out of her shaking hands. "You okay?"

She nodded then her eyes grew large a split second before both of them were knocked to the ground. Everything happened so fast that Keegan could barely process it. Ana screamed in agony and sank to the ground in front of him, a knife sticking out of her stomach.

****

Ana came awake inside some kind of medical center. At first she wasn't sure where she was until she caught Keegan's oak-and-spice scent nearby. Turning her head in the direction of his scent, she saw him sitting in an armchair, head back and eyes closed.

She went to sit up, and a sharp pain shot up her side, making her ease back down in the bed.

"Don't try to sit."

Keegan's sleep-hazed voice made her smile. "Once the Alpha, always the Alpha."

"I agree."

She jerked her gaze toward the sound of the voice at

the door, where two males entered. One of them was the male she fought the mutants with. She wasn't sure how, but she knew they were her brothers. Tears filled her eyes, and she blinked them away.

The taller one with midnight-black hair came toward her and held out his hand. "I'm Blaine and this," he gestured to the other male who approached, "is Alec."

She shook his hand, and a sense of peace, of home, warmed her heart. "Hi," she said, not really knowing what to say.

When Blaine pulled his hand back, he stared at her for a short, uncomfortable moment before saying, "You risked your life for Addyson and our father. As I understand it, that is the second time you helped our father out."

Our father. She knew he'd said the words twice deliberately. She peered over at Keegan, who still had his eyes shut, but she knew he wasn't asleep. He was listening to every word.

He looked so at ease, as though he had finally found that inner peace.

Studying his strong jaw line and straight black hair, she saw similarities to herself. She had his hair, but her eyes looked more like Blaine's.

"You and Blaine got your eyes from your mother," Keegan said without lifting his lashes.

Surprised, she cast a quick glance to Blaine. He smiled and said, "The Elder is telepathic."

She frowned and looked at her hands in her lap. "A mindbender?"

It was Alec who answered. "No. He can hear your thoughts. Many times it's not on purpose. He can tune them out but can't shut off the ability."

Keegan sat up in his chair, drawing her attention back to him. "I do have the ability to alter memories, but not control people's minds like Felix can do."

Relief floored her. She could deal with someone hearing her thoughts, but she couldn't live another day with someone who could control her every action. She speared a glance through the open doorway and caught Kieran walking toward her.

Keegan stood, stretched, and then said, "Blaine, Alec, and I have to go meet with the wolves. I'll be back to visit soon."

She nodded and watched the three males walk out of the room and Kieran enter. She smiled at him then frowned at his worried expression. "What is it?"

He came to her and brushed his knuckles down her cheek. "I can only stay for a moment. I should be at the same meeting."

Her heart shuddered. "Why? What's going on?"

He sighed and met her gaze. "If I know Keegan, he's planning on raiding the Onyx den."

"And you're just going to tell him where it is? What about Sable and Nigel?"

He leaned in and pressed his forehead to hers. "I warned Sable this would happen. Besides, she placed Nigel in a boarding school two weeks ago and told Felix it was to challenge the boy's intelligence."

He fell silent, and she wondered if this was the right thing to do. Yes, she hated Felix and everything he stood for. "Just promise me you won't tell me how many innocent lives were lost."

He pressed his lips to her temple and pulled pack. "I promise."

"Go meet with your Alphas."

"Ana? This isn't your fight. You're where you belong now, with family and a Pack that loves you."

She nodded, knowing he was right. Yet, she was confused and felt out of place. What if she'd escaped one hell just to enter into another?

CHAPTER FIFTEEN

They met in the conference room of the office building where the Alphas conducted official Pack business. Blaine sat at the head of the table. The spot Keegan had sat for as long as he was Alpha. It felt strange to not sit there.

"We can't just go charging into the den."

Keegan snapped his gaze to Blaine. "Yes, I can."

Blaine growled and ran a hand over his short black hair. "Okay stubborn-ass. You'll need backup. Alec, call in the strongest sentries and enforcers to go in."

Alec narrowed his eyes at Keegan and answered his brother. "Done. I'm going in, too."

Travis, Keegan's son-in-law, and Hayden, the wolf Marshal, threw in their bids to go with Keegan. Apparently he wasn't the only one who wanted the

Onyx Pack to go down.

And they would go down.

Keegan meet Luna's stare and raised a brow. If anyone beside himself had a personal vendetta against the Onyx Alpha, it was Luna. So, yeah, he wasn't at all surprised to see the longing in her eyes to go and give Felix what he deserved and then some.

However, old laws prevented one Alpha from attacking another or declaring war on another's Pack. It was kind of ironic that they sat here looking for loopholes in the laws while Felix disregarded them like last month's trash.

Jared appeared in the doorway with a book in hand and a smirk on his face. When he walked farther into the room, he set the large law book on the table for everyone to see. Pointing at a section, he read the last sentence, "In event that one Alpha outright attacks another, whether it be directly or indirectly, the Council of Elders must lay judgment upon said Alpha and his followers."

Jared raised his blue gaze to Keegan, satisfaction written all over the jaguar's face.

"What's the catch? Surely I alone can't make that call."

Jared straightened and nodded. "You're right. There needs to be a vote among the Elders, meaning there needs to be at least three."

Keegan sat back in his leather chair and studied the room around him just as Kieran walked in the room with Addyson close behind. Addyson held back, standing just inside the door. Keegan offered her a smile before meeting Kieran's gaze.

"Jared, refresh my memory on how to appoint a new Elder into the Council." Keegan felt his lips twitch at the suspicious look in Kieran's eyes.

Jared peered from Keegan to Kieran and laughed. "All he has to do is except your offer in front of witnesses. Kieran is eligible by default because he was a Marshal."

That was all Keegan needed to hear. "Kieran Michaels, I hereby appoint you as an Elder of Ashwood Falls. Do you accept?"

Kieran smiled. "I accept."

Jared nodded. "Great. I'll do the paperwork later and have both Blaine and Luna sign them. We still need a third. I suggest trying to find one outside the den."

Keegan nodded in agreement. He itched to get his hands on Felix and tear down his organization for good. "Kieran, what about the rebels you said lived inside the den? Will they be a problem?"

Kieran shook his head. "I informed the leader of the possibilities. She won't stand in our way. In fact, I believe they'll take the attack as an opportunity to make a clean break from the Pack."

Luna peered at Kieran and asked, "What do you know about the rebels? How many are there?"

Kieran shrugged. "There are a number of cells scattered over the U.S., both human groups and shifter groups. The shifters are a mix of breeds with the same goal, bring back order to the races and secure the secrecy of all shifters. The human rebels have only one goal: rid the world of all shifters."

Hayden growled low. "Fan-fucking-tastic. It isn't enough that Onyx wants to be top of the shifter food chain, but now we have to deal with human hate groups."

Luna clicked her tongue against the roof of her mouth and said, "I don't like, or trust, any group that tries to take the law into their own hands. Lord knows we've dealt with enough of that shit for the last two hundred years." She looked at Keegan and added, "We still need at least one more Elder."

Travis pushed off the wall where he was leaning. "You still have to make your status change to the Pack Network."

Keegan felt a grin forming on his lips. The Pack Network was an encrypted online community for shifter Packs across the world. He pulled out his phone and clicked on the app Dane had developed for easier access to the Network. Once logged into his profile, he sent his announcement.

I, Keegan Andrews, have retired my Alpha status. My eldest son, Blaine Andrews, has graciously accepted his new title of leopard Alpha of Ashwood Falls. I have also decided to recreate the Council of Elders as Elder of Ashwood and appointed Kieran Michaels as my second. I would like to put a call out to all other Elders to come forward and join the council because my first proposal is to lay judgment on Felix Darwin and the Onyx Pack for their blatant disregard of our laws.

It wasn't the most professional of addresses, but he'd never agreed to be professional. His closest friends and family could contest to that.

Putting his phone in his pocket, he said, "Now we wait. I just hope there are Elders out there."

Blaine stood up. "I don't know about you, but I'm going to enjoy my mates before we storm the enemy."

Mutters and teasing gestures filled the room as Blaine walked out. Travis was next to leave, and Keegan figured it was to get back to his pregnant mate, and Keegan's adopted daughter, Shay.

Soon everyone filed out leaving him, Jared, and Addyson. He looked from Addyson to Jared and asked, "What is this?"

Jared nodded toward Addyson. "She asked me to stay. Well, texted me and told me to stay after the meeting."

Addyson glanced at Keegan then averted her gaze to study the floor.

"Addy?"

She met his gaze and took a deep breath. "I want to see if Jared can unlock my memories."

Keegan looked at Jared. "You can do that, right?"

Jared drew his brows together in thought. "I've never tried. I mean I suppose I could, in theory." He turned to Addyson and asked, "Where do you want to do this?"

Hope lit up in her eyes, but quickly faded as fear crept in. "Um, I'd like to go to my home. It's familiar."

Keegan took her hand, trying to soothe the worry he could feel stirring inside her. He noticed how Jared's gaze lingered on his and Addyson's linked hands, but the jaguar didn't respond, just gave a short nod and said, "I can meet you two there in about twenty minutes."

After Jared left the conference room, Keegan drew her into him and kissed her forehead. "I'm proud of you for taking this step."

She sighed and pressed her cheek against his chest. "I need to know who my parents were, where I came from. Plus I'm stronger now thanks to you."

"I can't take credit. You are the one with the will and desire to heal, to live. I'm just enjoying watching you bloom and become the woman I know you are."

She lifted her head, met his eyes, and smiled. "Are you getting soft on me, my Alpha?"

He felt his lips twitch while his heart danced with a delight he hadn't felt since Cate. "Only for you, Addy. We must never speak of it in public."

She laughed then let out a squeal as he pulled her closer and captured her mouth with his.

****

Addyson had a million butterflies trapped inside her stomach. At least that was what it felt like as she paced her sunroom while waiting for Jared.

She felt Keegan watching in silence for several moments until he asked, "Are you sure about this?"

Addyson stopped pacing and faced him. "No. Maybe." She dropped her shoulders and wrapped her arms around her middle. "I want to remember my parents. I want to know if I had any siblings."

"Even if it causes you grief?"

She nodded. "Yes. Then at least I have a reason to grieve. Right now I have only you and Will. I have no past."

A rustle of clothing followed by Keegan's large arms wrapping around her from behind made her sigh. This male always knew exactly what she needed.

And why not? He was her mate and she, his.

Leaning back into his embrace, she took in the peaceful landscape of her backyard. Man, she was glad to be home. "It was nice of Shay to perform a cleansing ritual in the house."

Keegan kissed her temple. "Yes, and without being asked. I'd have to punish her when she was little to get her to clean her own room."

Addyson laughed, but it didn't ease her nervousness. She was almost afraid of returning to her home. There had been so many people inside her house the night Will stumbled through the wards and into her backyard, bringing rogues and mutants with him.

"Keegan?"

"Hmm?"

"Where is Will?"

"Alec took him to meet Rhea and then Sammie and Max." Keegan's tone was soft as though he was enjoying the quiet he had told her she'd given him.

Suddenly, Keegan stiffened, the calm leaving his body, but not in alarm. She knew he sensed someone coming to disturb their peace. Yet, he didn't draw away from her. He stayed right where he was with his arms around her, holding her close. A few moments later Jared entered the backyard. The butterflies stirred again. This time it felt as though they were trying to create a cyclone inside her belly.

Oh, God, she was going to be sick.

As Jared got closer, and she pushed down the crippling fear, she noticed he had on a pair of loose-fit blue jeans and a black T-shirt. His hair was damp and looked towel dried, nothing like the usual hairstyle she was used to seeing. Was this what he looked like when he wasn't working?

He opened the screen door and stepped inside, curiosity swirling in his expression as he met Keegan's gaze. Unease seeped through her, and she started to move out of Keegan's embrace, but he tightened his hold, keeping her in place.

She relaxed into his hold. They were mated now and she loved the male holding her and would do anything to keep him. That was why she needed to take this final step in healing. Nevin had urged her to ask Jared to unlock the memories her mind was protecting. Then Keegan insisted on it, but her leopard had given the final nudge. She had to do this no matter what memories were locked deep in her subconscious mind.

"Do you want to do this in here or outside?"

Jared's soft, yet deep, voice broke through her thoughts. She studied him for a brief moment then looked out into her backyard. "Outside. I can ground myself if needed."

Jared nodded and walked out the door, holding it open for her. Keegan kissed her neck, and she jumped. Damn she was nervous.

When Keegan released her, she stepped forward and carefully walked by Jared to avoid skin contact with him. She knew she'd have to touch him to unlock her buried memories, but right now she couldn't handle it.

Once on the grass, she slipped her shoes off and walked barefooted to the middle of the yard and sat with her legs folded under her. The males followed suit, Jared taking the spot in front of her and Keegan to her left.

She met Jared's cool blue eyes and smiled, but she knew it was a weak attempt. Jared smiled back, warm and inviting. It soothed her a little.

Jared cut a quick glance to Keegan then back to her before he asked, "Have you learned to build your shields?"

Addyson blinked and nodded. "How did you know?"

Keegan made a noise that sounded more like a muffled growl, catching Jared's attention. Jared studied the two of them for a long moment. Finally Keegan said, "Speak your mind, Jared."

Jared narrowed his eyes at the other male then focused on Addyson. "You can't read him."

She shook her head. "Not at all. Never have," she admitted, lifting her chin just a little.

Jared gave a short nod and held out his hands, palms up. "You can't use your shields. I have to be able to enter your mind to unlock your memories." When she nodded her understanding, he added, "My gift doesn't work without skin-to-skin contact."

She took a deep breath. "Yes, I know." She lifted her hands and held them just inches above his. "Any dark secrets you want to share before I touch you?"

He chuckled softly. "Sable Darwin is...was my mate and is hiding my son from me."

She stared at him. Was he joking? When his expression or his scent didn't change, she knew he wasn't kidding. They really were mates. "Were you bound? If so, who broke it?"

Jared let out a breath and closed his eyes. He had to know she'd see it, feel it, once their hands touched. His eyes opened, the blue a little darker than before, but it wasn't out of anger. No there was a stronger emotion in those blue depths.

"I can't do this. I can't subject you to the pain, to the darkness I've tried to bury. Yes, we were bonded and lived together in secret for about six months before I found out who she was."

Jared went to stand up, and without thinking about what she was doing, she grabbed his forearm to stop him. Flashes of images scrolled through her mind, bringing in a wave of emotions. First there was happiness then a feeling of betrayal and finally the agonizing pain of having his soul split in two when he broke the mating bond.

Just as fast as the images appeared, they vanished. She found herself sitting in Keegan's lap while he held her close to his chest. "What?" she tried to ask around the huge lump in her throat.

Keegan brushed his fingers through her hair. "You started crying uncontrollably."

She took in a shaky breath and looked around for Jared. She found him standing a few feet away, staring off into the forest surrounding her home. She wiggled out of Keegan's lap and was glad when he didn't protest.

She walked over and stood next to Jared, leaving about a foot between them. Even though the worst was over for her, she didn't think Jared knew that. So she put some space between them.

After what felt like hours of silence, she said, "Sable isn't like her father."

Jared snorted. "She's everything like him."

Addyson clicked her tongue in irritation and turned to face his profile. "She's the leader of a rebel shifter group that is plotting against Felix."

Jared jerked around and stared at her. "What?"

Addyson rolled her eyes. "You heard me. If you don't believe me, then ask Kieran."

Jared cast a glance to Keegan. "You knew about this?"

Keegan shrugged. "I was going to tell you when the time was right. I wasn't sure how you'd take it. She's still an outlaw going against the Council of Elders and taking the law into her own hands."

Addyson placed her hand on Jared T-shirt over his heart, drawing his gaze back to her. "I still need your help to unlock my memories. It's the only way I can have closure."

Jared glanced back at Keegan still sitting in the grass watching them then nodded. "Let's get this over with."

This time when Addyson sat back on the ground she closed her eyes and grounded her energy to the earth below her. When she opened her eyes, she saw Jared patiently waiting. "I'm ready," she said, feeling much better connected to the earth. It wouldn't dampen the pain or the flow of emotions, but it helped her relax to know she was grounded. She could use the earth to push away the ugliness.

Jared raised a hand slowly and laid it on her cheek. The new visions didn't instantly appear, but when they did, they made her giggle.

A very young Cameron was crawling out of her

bedroom window. When she'd made it out, she turned and ran smack into Jared. "Where are you going?" Jared asked, his tone firm like a father would use with his disobedient daughter.

Cameron didn't miss a beat. She crossed her arms and looked him in the eye. "I dropped something out my window."

Jared growled. "Try again."

The vision vanished, bringing her back to the present. She smiled and said, "Cameron was a handful."

Jared laughed. "Yes, she was. Can we start now?"

Addyson nodded. When Jared touched her cheek again, he didn't give her ability time to dig into his past again. She felt a nudge inside her mind, warm yet soothing. She could feel Jared's mind mingling with hers as, one-by-one, memories of her life before captivity spilled into her mind.

The images started to rush threw her mind faster than she could process them. She caught glimpses of her parents' faces, smiling and so much in love. Her mother had blond hair, like Addyson and crystal blue eyes. Her father had light brown hair and violet eyes. Addyson's heart filled with the love she felt for the two people who'd never know if their daughter was safe. Hot fat tears rolled down her cheeks.

Then images of the den she lived in, and a few friends whose names she couldn't recall, but figured they'd come in time. There was so much to try to process all at once, so she forced her eyes open and peered at Jared.

Jared removed his hand from her cheek, and she flung her arms around his neck. He stiffened then relaxed and hugged her back. "Thank you."

CHAPTER SIXTEEN

Keegan sat on the sofa in Addyson's living room as she flew around looking for a notebook and pen. He'd never seen her excited. She was actually a little jittery, as though she didn't know what to do with herself.

She laughed as she found a notebook and came to sit next to him. She took a deep breath and opened a hardback notebook with blue butterflies on the cover and stared at it.

"What's wrong?" he asked.

She dropped her shoulders and peered over at him. "I don't know where to start."

He held in a smile and ran his knuckles down her cheek. "You have a lifetime to shift through your memories. Don't try to do it all in one day."

Her smile reached her eyes, the same eyes that had

held so much darkness they made him want to rip Felix apart inch by agonizing inch. Now the violet depths held a light he hadn't seen before. She had hope.

He cupped the back of her neck and drew her in so he could claim her lips with his. She came willingly and opened for him. He slipped his tongue inside her mouth, finding hers. He heard the notebook and pen fall to the floor as she twisted to climb up his body and straddle him.

Groaning, he slid one of his hands under her shirt, and the other he fisted in her hair. He broke the kiss and pulled back to peer into her desire-filled gaze.

God, he loved her.

The admission wasn't a surprise. His leopard had known all along. It had just taken the man too long to see it.

His phone rang, drawing a growl from him and making Addyson laugh. He pulled the cell out and answered with a sharp, "Yeah."

Blaine's amusement filtered through the line. "Bad time?"

Keegan was not amused. "Speak."

"Still barking orders like an Alpha." Blaine's voice faded a little as if he'd pulled the phone away from his face, and then Keegan heard Max's voice right before Blaine came back to the phone. "Travis got a few replies to your broadcast."

A thrill spiked through Keegan at the possibility that Onyx could finally get what they deserved. "No shit? How many?"

"Three other Elders stepped forward and await your appointments to the Council. I've called a meeting, and Alec is setting up a videoconference. Meet me at the office in five." Blaine hung up, and Keegan met Addyson's gaze.

Her expression told him she understood. He also knew she was still searching through her lost memories. He kissed her lips and asked, "Are you okay?"

She smiled again, but this time it didn't quite reach her eyes. "Yes, just worried." She nibbled on her bottom lip and averted her gaze.

He gently took her chin and directed her gaze back to his. "This is a good thing for all breeds of shifters. We may not be able to completely stop Onyx, but we will definitely leave a message that we aren't sitting back waiting anymore."

She relaxed a little and pushed off his lap. "I know. It's a positive step that the den and other Packs need right now."

God, he loved her. His strong, submissive, beautiful snow leopard.

He stood and pulled her to him. "What will you do while I'm gone?"

She nipped at his chin playfully. "I thought I'd go to the nursery and talk with Rhea and visit with the kids. Without my gloves."

His chest filled with pride for her. "Going to work on building your shields?"

She nodded. "Yep."

He smiled. "Be careful. Those kids know how to put spells on you that will make you do anything they want."

Laughing, she slapped at his chest. "They only do that with you."

He kissed her forehead and stepped away. "I'll see you tonight."

A shy smile crossed her face. "I'm looking forward to it."

****

Five minutes later, Keegan sat to the right of Blaine at the large conference table with Jared and Kieran looking at the three Elders that had joined the meeting via video feed, two males and one female, each from a different Pack and each a different breed of shifter. Keegan had worked with each of them over the years.

What surprised him was the bear, Donovan Parker. Bears tended to stay to themselves and almost never got involved in Council business.

Donovan was a large biker type. He had long blond hair that hung loose around his shoulder and a full beard that extended about four inches below his chin.

Keegan nodded. "Donovan."

The bear sat back in his chair and gave a short nod. "It's good to see you again, Keegan."

Keegan focused on the other male, a puma and ex-Alpha of Crimson Stone—the puma Pack about fifty miles south of Ashwood Falls. "Ryker."

Ryker Stone was the typical alpha male with light brown hair and dimpled cheeks. He looked much too young by human standard to buy alcohol despite being over six hundred years old. He only stood about five nine, but carried a power inside him that rivaled most Alphas Keegan knew. He was forced into the position by his father, right before his father died. Since he was the only child of the Alpha pair, he couldn't refuse the power transfer. As Keegan understands it, the Alpha magick won't go to anyone outside the Alpha family as long as there's a blood relative alive.

The puma nodded his greeting, and Keegan moved to the third Elder, Micaela Callahan. She was the retired Marshal of the tiger Pack in the mountains of Virginia. Tall and exotic, she had straight black hair and dark brown eyes.

Micaela didn't waste time with niceties. She cut right to the point of the meeting and threw in her bid. "I want to see the Onyx Pack go down, and I'm happy to serve on the Council to see that happen."

"The tigress has claws." Donovan chuckled.

Micaela just shrugged and replied, "I'm not afraid to use them, bear."

Before Donovan had a chance to bite out a retort, Blaine cut in. "We're here for a reason. If you don't mind, I'd like to stop wasting my time and get this done so I can go back to my mates and kids."

Micaela's lips twitched in amusement. "Keegan, your son hasn't fallen far from the tree." When Blaine let a growl in warning, she rolled her eyes and continued. "I accept the invitation to take a seat on the Council of Elders. I vow to cast judgment fairly and in the best interest of all shifter Packs under our jurisdiction."

One by one, the other two males, Kieran, and Keegan spoke their vows similar to Micaela's. When finished, Keegan nodded to Jared, and the jaguar signed as a witness on the contract he'd drafted earlier that would legally bond the five of them together as the Council of the Elders.

Blaine met Luna's eye for a brief moment then addressed the group. "Jared found a clause in the law that provides the loophole we need to go after Felix and his followers."

Ryker, Donovan, and Micaela sat up straighter in their chairs, interest and eagerness crossing their faces.

Jared spoke up to explain the clause. "It says if an Alpha has directly or indirectly attacked another Alpha, the Council can vote on a punishment."

Micaela grinned. "Well then. Let's go get the bastard and put him down."

Ryker and Donovan chimed in at the same time with their support. Keegan didn't have to ask what Felix had done to them. He knew. Each of their Packs had been attacked much like Ashwood and MoonRiver was. Lives of people they loved and protected had been lost to the greed of an insane, power-hungry leopard.

Ryker growled. "I vote to go bring him in for a very public trial."

Donovan nodded. "I second that."

Keegan raised a brow to Micaela, and she let out a breath. "I'd rather kill him on the spot, but, yes, we need to bring him in for trail."

Kieran raised his hand, putting in his vote. Keegan closed the meeting after putting in his vote and sharing the plan to go into the Onyx den to arrest Felix and his Marshals. The mutants weren't considered "natural born shifters" under law and, therefore, were not protected by it.

They would die on spot.

CHAPTER SEVENTEEN

Keegan, with Kieran on one side and Hayden on the other, came to a stop at the wards surrounding what Kieran said was the Onyx's land. Keegan clenched his jaw, not believing just how close the rogues were to his home.

Kieran said the den was inside the mountain they now stood on, and in order to get inside, they had to take a very steep and narrow path down a ravine. It wasn't the only entrance, but it was the only one that enabled them to get around the wards with enough time to get inside the den.

Keegan started down the path first against Hayden's request to let him test the ground. Hayden's growl and the sounds of his footsteps on his heels amused Keegan. When would the wolf Marshal learn? Keegan hadn't followed his or Blaine's advice on safety when he was Alpha, and he damn sure wasn't going to do it as an Elder either.

Once at the bottom of the ravine, Keegan scanned the area and waited for Felix's soldiers and mutants to charge them. No one jumped out at them. Hayden and Kieran stepped up next to him. "Everything is too quiet."

Kieran marched forward, forcing Keegan and Hayden to follow. "Yeah. Something is up."

"Keegan." Travis's voice entered his mind. The tracker had taken a small team to the main entrance of the den. "This feels like a trap to me. I think he's been tipped off."

"My thoughts exactly," Keegan replied back telepathically then focused on Kieran. "How much do you trust Sable?"

Kieran's mouth thinned. "For her sake, I hope she hasn't betrayed me or Ana. But I trust my gut, and she's against her father's twisted mission as much as we are."

Keegan wasn't so sure. He didn't know Sable and had never come into connect with her. He did know, however, that she was Jared's mate. Keegan hoped for Jared's sake that Sable really was on the right team.

"Keep your eyes and ears open. We're not as alone as it appears." Keegan moved toward an opening in the mountain wall. He entered into a tunnel. He blinked several times to allow his eyes to adjust to the lack of light as he proceeded down the tunnel and toward the low hum of other people's thoughts.

Several feet inside, Keegan saw a dim light ahead, stopped, and held a hand up. Kieran and Hayden stopped beside him.

"What is it?" Hayden asked.

Keegan listened. The hum he'd thought was the side

effect of his telepathic gift was all wrong. The sound was more like soft mutters, and they were not in his head. "This is definitely a setup."

Kieran sniffed the air and growled. "The mountain is rigged to blow."

The three of them turned to the exit of the tunnel just as an explosion went off, shaking the mountain. Keegan hit the floor and cover his head. Rock and dirt caved in around them. When the dust cleared, Keegan stood and cursed. The entrance to the tunnel was blocked, forcing them to go farther inside the den.

"Trapped like rats," Hayden growled out.

Kieran pushed at them to move. "Keep going. Our only way out is up."

They ran up the tunnel until it split into two sections. Kieran pointed. "Go right."

Keegan didn't hesitate. He rushed right and ran into dead end. "What the fuck, Kieran?"

Kieran turned on his phone to light up the space and point it to the wall. He fingered a few bricks, and a door opened. Light spilled out into the tunnel, and Keegan could tell the room was a bedroom.

Keegan followed Kieran inside with Hayden close behind. That was when he noticed the room was the Alpha's chambers. Yet, he didn't scent Felix within.

As if knowing what he was thinking, Kieran said, "This was Sable's apartment. Felix thought he was too good to stay here with the soldiers so close by."

Keegan nodded. It sounded like the arrogant ass. "Or he didn't want anyone knowing what his plans were." Felix trusted no one. Not even his Marshal and enforcers.

Another explosion sounded off from somewhere inside the den. The ground shook, throwing Keegan and the other two males off balance.

"There must be charges all over the den," Hayden said.

Keegan agreed. "And they are most likely set to go off one by one until the mountain caves in."

Keegan rushed through the apartment and out into a hallway. "Which way, Kieran?"

Kieran pushed past and lead them down the hall then turned left to a large community center. It reminded him of an indoor courtyard much like the one Ashwood had in the center of the den. Kieran pointed straight ahead, and Keegan smiled.

Large double doors marked the den's main entrance. They took a step toward them then stopped as four very large half-man, half-wolf mutants stepped in their path.

Hayden growled. "Looks like the gatekeepers have arrived."

Keegan sent out a mental call to Travis. "We're at the front exit and need backup."

The mutants charged them. Keegan ducked a blow and kicked out a leg to trip the half-wolf. The creature stumbled, giving Keegan the time he needed to draw his gun and fire.

"They aren't as fast as we are. Use your speed," he called out to the others.

The next instant Keegan was hit in the side by another mutant. They fell to the floor and slid until Keegan's back slammed against the rock wall. Pain shot up his spine, and he gritted his teeth and tried to breathe through it. He met the fierce stare of the creature now holding him by the neck and reached inside his mind with his own.

Keegan used the healing side of his telepathy to alter the mutant's thought patterns. He wasn't sure it'd work. It was a little like mindbending, except, when Keegan did it, he was left drained. A side effect he'd gladly submit to if it meant saving his Pack mates from blowing up along with this damned mountain.

He knew the moment he had control over the mutant's mind. His blank stare became that of recognition. For a split moment, Keegan saw who the man had been before becoming the creature stuck in mid-shift. A human male fugitive on the run from the law.

Well, at least Keegan would be doing both worlds a favor.

"Attack the other mutants."

The creature tilted his head then released Keegan's neck. Keegan slid to the ground, and his legs and arms felt useless. Keegan watched as the mutant grabbed another one and tossed him across the room then attacked the other one.

Kieran and Hayden looked stunned and a little confused. They turned to Keegan just as the front doors blew open and Travis, with his team of sentries, stormed in.

Hayden was the first to reach Keegan. "What the hell happened?"

"I...took control of...his mind," Keegan spoke through gulps of air. Fuck. That had taken more out of him than he expected. "Have to go. Bombs."

Hayden wrapped an arm around his waist, placed his shoulder under Keegan's arm, and lifted him up. "Everyone out. The place is rigged to blow."

Everything started to grow dark, but Keegan fought to stay alert, to make sure his males got out safely. He was losing the battle as the last of his energy left his body and his mind shut down in exhaustion.

CHAPTER EIGHTEEN

Keegan opened his eyes unsure where he was and what had woken him. After scanning the room, he relaxed and smiled. Addyson's room. It was the only thing that made sense. Her scent was everywhere, and the cloak she wore in public was draped over the chair next to the dresser.

Sitting up, he half expected to be hit by dizziness, but it didn't come. In fact, he felt great. He stood and regretted his last thought. The room spun, and he had to spread his arms out to balance himself. He took a deep breath then a small step. The dizziness went away, and he was able to make it to the door without falling on his face.

What the hell?

"Dad! What are you doing?" Shay rushed down the

hall toward him. The sundress she wore showed off her small protruding belly. His grandchild.

He reached for her and drew her in for a hug. "I'm fine, princess."

"You need to rest."

He kissed her forehead, let her go, and walked down the stairs to the living room where he heard the voices of his sons as well as the wolves. Why the hell was everyone in Addyson's house?

When he entered the living room, he stopped in his tracks. Addyson held Max in her arms as she stood next to Luna, and Luna's hand rested on her forearm. The women were talking quietly and laughing.

His heart swelled, washing away the initial fear at seeing them touching. Then he had a thought. Had Max been able to heal Addyson's sensitivity to touch? It was possible. The kid was an Empath and a Healer. Even at his young age, his powers were strong.

Max twisted his head in Keegan's direction and started wiggling until Addyson put him down. The three-year-old ran to Keagan and held his arms up. "Up, Grandpa."

Keegan lifted him up and smiled. "What are you up to, little man?"

Max smiled shyly and said, "I healed Addy."

Keegan moved his gaze to Addyson, who was walking toward him now. She smiled at him and ran a hand down Max's back. "My heart has been stolen by another."

Grinning, Keegan shrugged. "I can't compete with this one."

She laughed. "Our little Healer is amazing. I mean, Ana had already showed me how to create a shield that worked and with my memories unlocked it became easier for me to build shields and hold them, but Max just touched my temples, and everything snapped in place. Now I don't have to focus as much to shield against others. I'm also gaining more control over my gift."

Keegan leaned in but jumped when Max yelled, "Mommy!" Then he wiggled until Keegan set him on his feet. Keegan looked at the door and saw Graham and Cameron walk in. Cameron caught Max as he jumped at her.

Shay patted him on the back. "Go sit. Blaine wants to brief us before we have dinner. I'm going to check on Rhea in the kitchen. I thought I saw Alec go that way."

Keegan chuckled and watched Shay dart off. Addyson laughed and tugged him to the sofa. When he sat with his mate snuggled in next to him, Blaine started filling him and everyone in on Onyx and the Council.

"Hayden said the onyx den was empty, expect for a couple of crypt keepers."

Everyone laughed, and Hayden spoke up to correct Blaine. "I said gatekeepers."

Blaine's lips twitched. "Same, same. Anyway, Kieran doesn't believe it was an actual setup. He seems to think it was more bad timing on our part. I agree. But I also think Felix was tipped off somehow and decided to go on the run."

Keegan grunted in disgust. "Damn coward. He can't run forever."

Hayden spoke next. "He sure can't. We'll give him a little rope and let him think we're as dumb as he thinks we are. In the meantime, I got a couple of leads on a human rebel group called Shield. Their HQ is a few miles outside Memphis, Tennessee. I'm heading out there first thing in the morning, set up shop, and see what I can dig up."

Luna didn't look pleased. "Take Tanner with you."

Hayden smirked. "Mom, that sounded so mom-like. 'Take your little brother with you.'"

Luna growled. "You know what I mean. His telekinesis will come in handy."

Hayden walked over to her and picked her up in a tight hug. Keegan could see her smile, even though she tried to hide it from her son.

Keegan squeezed Addyson closer and met her gaze. Her violet eyes held so much light now, so much hope for the future. "I love you, and I'm so happy to be your bonded mate for the rest of our existence."

Her eyes teared up, and she threw her arms around his neck. "I love you, too. I'm yours... forever."

She kissed him, and their souls reached for each other and twisted together, strengthening the connection that bound them as lifelong mates.

The End

ABOUT THE AUTHOR

Lia Davis is a mother to two young adults and two very special kitties, a wife to her soul mate, a paranormal romance author, graphic designer, and co-owner to Fated Desires Publishing, LLC. She and her family live in Northeast Florida battling hurricanes and very humid summers. But it's her home and she loves it!

An accounting major, Lia has always been a dreamer with a very activity imagination. The wheels in her head never stop. She ventured into the world of writing and publishing in 2008 and loves it more than she imagined. Writing and designing are stress relievers that allow her to go off in her corner of the house and enter into another world that she created, leaving real life where it belongs.

Her favorite things are spending time with family, traveling, reading, writing, chocolate, coffee, nature and hanging out with her kitties.

CPSIA information can be obtained at www.ICGtesting.com
Printed in the USA
LVOW05s1743110514

385318LV00005B/928/P